Dedalus Europe
General Editor: Timothy Lane

CW00546330

Bestseller

Beka Adamashvili

Bestseller

translated by Tamar Japaridze

Dedalus

This book is published with the support of the Writers' House of Georgia and Arts Council England.

WRITERS'
HOUSE
OF GEORGIA

Published in the UK by Dedalus Limited
24-26, St Judith's Lane, Sawtry, Cambs, PE28 5XE
email: info@dedalusbooks.com
www.dedalusbooks.com

ISBN printed book 978 1 912868 36 0
ISBN ebook 978 1 912868 50 6

Dedalus is distributed in the USA & Canada by SCB Distributors
15608 South New Century Drive, Gardena, CA 90248
email: info@scbdistrutors.com   web: www.scbdistributors.com

Dedalus is distributed in Australia by Peribo Pty Ltd
58, Beaumont Road, Mount Kuring-gai, N.S.W. 2080
email: info@peribo.com.au

First published by Dedalus in 2020

Printed and bound in the UK by Clays Elcograf, S.p.A
Typeset by Marie Lane

THE AUTHOR

Born in 1990, Beka Adamashvili is a postmodern Georgian author, blogger, screenwriter, and Creative Director at an advertising agency. In 2011 he graduated from Caucasus School of Media at Caucasus University with a BA in Journalism and Social Sciences.

In 2014 his first novel *Bestseller* was published. It became a real bestseller in Georgia and was on the shortlist for the best debut novel at the SABA Literary Awards and as the best novel at the Tsinandali Awards. It also got a special prize at the Iliauni Literary Awards.

In 2018 Beka Adamashvili's second postmodern novel *Everybody Dies in This Novel* was published. It won an EU prize.

THE TRANSLATOR

Tamar Japaridze is a highly acclaimed Georgian translator and academic. She was the winner of the SABA Literary Prize in 2016 for the best translation of the year.

She has translated over thirty literary works from English into Georgian, including authors such as William Shakespeare, Rudyard Kipling, Harold Pinter, John Fowles, Henry Miller, Arundati Roy, Irvine Welsh, Bernardine Evaristo, Margaret Atwood and Kazuo Ishiguro.

To trees
as compensation for the insignificant damage
caused by using paper for this dedication.

CONTENTS

Quasi-preface

I can hardly think of anyone who is fond of reading prefaces, and even more so writing them. It's because the majority of prefaces are as long as the 21st night in December, as obligatory as complimenting each other at banquets, and as dull as the midnight TV programmes.

As for this one, by good luck it is short and does not provide any space for such lofty statements as: *The Author's style is saturated with extreme lightness and flexibility...; We should also note his expertly veiled symbolism, in which...; In the eclectic nature of the protagonist one can trace the embryo of moderate sadness...* et cetera. Firstly, because this book does not carry a deep and profound meaning; secondly, it is not loaded with ideological symbols the greatness of which is often incomprehensible to everyone, even to the authors themselves.

I must also warn you right at the start that you are not going to come across dirty words, pornographic scenes, or such shocking tricks which later make the authors measure the level of disreputability of the expressions used in their address. However, in this book you will find drawings and dialogues that (if not completely, then partially, at least) will compensate for the painful deficiencies mentioned above. On the whole, the novel is a light and enjoyable piece and, according to the rough calculation of the Author, can be easily read in 6325 breaths.

A couple of words about the locations in *Bestseller*: part of the action takes place in France. Selection of the country in the given context was purely conditional, as it was based on the phonetic characteristics of the protagonist's name – Pierre Sonnage. As for the second part, it unfolds in Literary Hell, and *since it is easier to draw a devil than a rooster* (as everyone has seen the latter and no one the former), it was much easier for the Author to cope with its description.[1]

Well, what else can I say? Welcome your eyes to Literary Hell!

---

1 Initially, the Author was not going to paraphrase any "wise words" in the preface, but Confucius' comparison of a devil and a rooster (the symbols of Hell and France) fitted into the comparative description of these two locations so well that he couldn't help doing so (embarrassed A/N).

*'And Mahalalel lived after he begat Jared
eight hundred and thirty years,
and begat sons and daughters.'*
Genesis 5:16

'So they all ate and were filled.'
Mark 6:42

*' '
*

James Joyce, *'Ulysses'*,
after every declarative sentence.[2]

---

2 These quotations have nothing to do with the events unfolding further. The Author simply tried to keep pace with popular trend and thereby create the illusion that deep wisdom is embedded in his book (A/N).

I

PR-Step
or
Oops! – Straight into Hell...

Pierre Sonnage firmly decided to commit suicide on his 33rd birthday. His motivation was not banal at all, I mean he hadn't caught his bride and the best man making love before the wedding; he hadn't gradually lost everything – his head, hopes and the last shirt – in a gambling house; he had never gone so deep into the existential problems as to be dragged into a swamp of vanity; neither was he seriously in debt to anyone except humankind for building a house, planting a tree and fathering a single son. In fact, when planning the suicide, its mission was far more idealistic than the mere prospect of solving the eternal dilemma of the immortality of the soul.

The thing is that Pierre Sonnage was a writer! Maybe unknown and not even socially active, but still. He belonged to the category of the creative individuals who prefer writing many books to reading them. Consequently, he had already published a lot of short stories and even four thick books. In some way he resembled Rubens for being fond of creating massive and heavy pieces. Nevertheless, literary gourmets rated his 'heavy' creations as 'easily digestible'. On the whole, the appraisal was not bad, but the rating didn't seem favourable to Pierre since standing on the same platform with Houellebecq, Le Clézio, and Beigbeder wasn't easy for him. Moreover, there were only a dozen readers at the presentation of his last book. True, he was not planning a grand presentation but we must admit that having a crowd of only twelve readers at the age of 33 is not a big number.

That, of course, could be explained easily: Pierre whole-heartedly believed that 'society was not ready to accept and appreciate his brilliant ideas'. So, in order to guide it to the true path, he had 'to take an effective step'. It was then that the idea of committing suicide, which gave rise to the whole complicated story, occurred to him…

(As Pierre Sonnage commits suicide at the end of this chapter, the Author did not consider it necessary to describe his appearance or personal traits at this point.)

Oh yes, Pierre decided to sacrifice himself to his creative life, as he knew that death has one immortal feature – it boosts respect.[3] Suicide was the only way for him to achieve eternal glory, because he knew another proven maxim[4] too: a man had to die to gain a deathless fame.

As one can commit suicide more or less only once in life, he wanted the event to happen with dignity and pomp. Therefore, he began to prepare for it far in advance. He refused to use the rope from the very start, since the rope which he had found in his closet was just as worn out as the method itself of committing suicide by hanging. He rejected the idea of shooting himself for the same reason (besides, he would die with fear before pulling the trigger). What's more important, he was absolutely sure that his brains deserved to be kept in a better place (say a glass container with a special liquid, proudly exposed in a museum) than on an ordinary wall. He even had thought of taking 33 sleeping pills, but later realised that after the autopsy nobody would be able to count the amount of the pills, and this smart symbolism would remain an eternal secret for the history of world literature. True, he could indicate it in his suicide note, but the sentence 'I'm 33 now, so I've decided to take 33 sleeping pills' would sound pretty odd, and he would rather die than write such rubbish!

There were myriads of other methods of committing suicide: demonstrative self-immolation in Rouen Square, jumping from the stream of life into the stream of the Seine, tasting raw fugu-fish, taking a loan from a bank or just jumping

---

3 He even wrote in one of his novels: 'If we showed our respect towards people as generously as we do posthumously, they would live a much longer and happier life.'

4 The Author could here use the synonymous words, such as 'truth', 'wisdom', 'axiom', etc. But as he is a maximalist, he decided to pretend to be more intellectual (note of the intel. Auth.)

under the train with his own books in his hand, thus attracting the passengers' attention with his aggressive advertising or with a desperate scream.

However, since Pierre believed that he contemplated the future standing on Newton's shoulders,[5] he decided to look death in the eye from a maximum height. Naturally, he rejected the moon and Everest at once; Everest because it was far away and the moon because it was even farther. Besides, even if his body was ever discovered, it was unlikely that anyone would considered a French writer who turned into a satellite or froze in the deep snows of Everest a suicide. So, with a cold mind and a warm heart, Pierre chose a height which he could reach quite easily.

Thus, on the day of his 33rd anniversary, he found himself in Dubai – the city built out of almost nothing – to build his own future out of almost nothing as well…

(Based on the fact that the Author hates depicting landscapes as his memory always delicately refuses to recall the beautiful words concerning the details of reliefs and bas-reliefs, he omits the description of any Dubai sights. As for the Burj Khalifa, it's easier to find its image on google than read its description which would take three pages at least.)

And lo, Pierre saw the Burj Khalifa with his own eyes, stepped into the lift with his own feet, pressed the button of the highest

---

5 In order to prove that the Author's knowledge of the word "maxim" was not accidental, here he paraphrases the famous expression by Isaac Newton: 'If I have seen further than the others, it is by standing on the shoulders of giants.'

available floor with his own finger, and felt the increasing pressure with his own ears while going up.

"Everyone has their own Calvary," he said to a 22-year-old girl in the lift, who got confused, left on the 28th floor, and probably thought for a while about what she had heard. Nothing significant, that might have changed Pierre's life, had happened after that, I mean, a glamorous woman didn't appear who would first stop Pierre in his tracks and then stop the lift; neither had the electricity been cut off, which would be a sign from above.

It was ascending for such a long time that Pierre even yawned three times, managed to take four selfies, hummed his favourite tune again and again, composed the plot of a new novel in his mind, and imagined the sentimental text (about the ruthless world) that would occur to him during his free fall. In the end, he comforted himself with the assumption that descending would take him much less time.

Psychologists claim (or some people claim that they claim) that when looking down from a height, one feels an overwhelming desire of performing a swan dive. This was not the case with Pierre. Moreover, if not for that damn PR, he would never undertake the *salto mortale*. Nevertheless, imagining the pinnacle of his glory at the pinnacle of architecture, he took a PR-step towards the void without giving it much thought…

…The flight turned out to be so long that on his way to the ground he first believed in Galileo's theory of falling objects, then in God, and in the end, when he approached the pavement with outstretched arms, he got thoroughly convinced of the infallibility of Newton's law of gravitation…

II

What the Hell Is Going on?

Pierre was always irritated by outdated idiomatic and often idiotic expressions. He preferred writing: *Her voice was sweet as November* rather than referring to the uniqueness of the vocal cords of the sirens whose vocals no one has ever heard; describing beauty, he avoided the word 'angelic' by saying: *beautiful as her own reflection*, since neither do angels pamper us with a frequent exposition of their appearance.

Nevertheless, when he opened his eyes after landing, what he felt could be described as 'the hellish heat'. He thought he would see a traditional picture of the hospital lights flickering on the ceiling, but alas!

Despite the fact that he fell from the 147th floor, he was lying on the ground healthy, and the gates in front of him did not resemble the doors to the intensive care unit.

So he got to his feet pretty amazed. The huge gates were inserted into the triumphal arch, and the long, high fence on both sides of it was lined with black obelisks. Strange silence reigned all around. A middle-aged man dressed in the well-forgotten style of medieval clothing stood smiling at the gates. Next to him lay a huge dog tied with a speckled band. From time to time, the dog emitted fire from its mouth leaving a scarlet trace in the air.

"Why art thou frightened? This hound's not cruel,
Sir Conan Doyle hath made him look like this;
He's an intern, Cerberus is on vacation," the man addressed Pierre from a distance with a soothing Italian accent, and then decided to make his next sentence more neutral as his manner of speaking might sound a little comical for the 21st-century writer.

Pierre scratched his head. He always did so when he was perplexed, and at that very moment he was indeed as perplexed as James Cook, who realised that the Hawaiian Aborigines were about to cook not *for him* but *him himself.* "I'm probably going to wake up now, and it's going to end banally," Pierre thought, and since in our dreams we are all more courageous than in reality, he boldly stepped towards the Italian.

Besides the man and the dog, at the gates stood a device in the shape of a white frame. It was an apparatus of the firm 'MEPHISTAPPLE' with a logo of a snake curled round a twice-bitten apple.

(Here the poor Author thinks that he has discovered an outstanding allusion.)

"This is the hope detector. We try to keep up, or rather walk hand in hand with modern technology," the Italian said, swiped a finger over the screen of the device and removed the block. "*Vivere militare est...*[6] So, if you have some kind of hope, you should abandon it here, before you enter."

"What do you mean?" Pierre guessed that he could no longer guess anything.

"I mean I hope that now you are already absolutely hopeless."

"Well, right you are, I'm hopeless even for my readers," Pierre smiled and decided to assent to this self-proclaimed dream, "All that I had, I left behind, um... in my previous life, Signore..."

"Alighieri, Dante Alighieri," the man clarified and dialled the code 1984 on the electric display to open the gates. "Welcome to Literary Hell!"

***

The hope that was 'left behind' justified itself indeed.

Speaking tripe, Pierre did not even dream of such popular love and admiration. A few sentimental statements and stories proved to be quite enough for tremendous acclaim: the effective headline: 'Unpromising step of a promising writer'; the words

---

6 *Vivere militare est...* (Lat.) – 'To live is to fight'. Despite the fact that neither this nor the other expressions that follow fit in the contexts very well, the Latin maxims, to the Author's mind, add some splendour to his narrative.

of the next door neighbour uttered with a deliberately surprised face and cautious scepticism: 'Lately he looked so happy…'; 'The great sorrow' of the President (read from the sheet of previously written paper) in connection with 'the great loss…'; and a dozen more yellow versions, such as: 'Actually, he was murdered'; 'Actually, he had an unlucky love affair' (and the journalists even found a certain Victoria whom 'Pierre had kissed twice – with the interval of three seconds – on the right corner of the upper lip seven years before'); 'He was gay, and Victoria was actually Victor'; 'It seems, he knew several state secrets', and so on and so forth. All in all, all roads led to *Roamin' in the Gloamin'* with Pierre on people's mind.

Newspapers echoed the pulsating television commentary eagerly: 'A prose writer who died poetically,' one of them wrote, although what was poetic in falling from a great height and hitting the forehead directly on the asphalt was known only to the author of the article. 'His books are the showers that irrigate our minds devastated by everyday worries,' an elderly critic admitted. 'Pierre suffered from altophobia,[7] otherwise he would have reached creative heights,' a self-satisfied writer acknowledged. 'If he had lived centuries before, Napoleon would have uttered before he departed: France, army, head of the army, Josephine, Pierre…' a well-known literary critic asserted and thought that he would have written a more competent conclusion if he had read at least one book by Pierre.

Readers, too, were filled with such immeasurable

---

7 The Author knows that the majority of readers will be reluctant to check the meaning of this word, so he defines it himself – altophobia is an abnormal fear of heights.

enthusiasm that the shelves allotted for Pierre's books were instantly emptied. Social networks were overloaded with comments in which Pierre, decorated with many smileys, was referred to as 'our contemporary Proust/Sartre/Flaubert/Mérimée, etc.'; 'a Caryatid which supported French literature'; 'a literary juggler playing with words', 'a genius whose books don't need a bookmark', and a thousand other appraisals like that. A lot of hearts, repeated kisses and other emoji of admiration were added to the verbal grief in such amounts that one would think the whole country was swept by massive necrophilia. People were worried, people were weeping, people were changing their profile pictures with Pierre's. So Pierre's image was getting from better to best.

One way or another, with a single step ahead Pierre achieved what he could not in all of his 33 years – *he was deified.*

III

Lucy, etc.

"As I've told you, this is Literary Hell," Dante began in about the same tone as the public speaker who draws with a marker on the whiteboard and thinks that he is cleverer than his listeners. "It turns out that all circles of Hell are broad comedy, and Hell is not as scary as I thought. Frankly speaking, I would choose heaven for climate and Hell for companionship.[8] The main drawback here is that writers are punished for their literary sins, that is, they suffer in the same way as readers do while reading their books…"

8 Here the Author must remind Dante that when quoting other authors, copyright should be taken into account!

"Oh…" Pierre thought, as due to the accelerated pace of Dante's speech, he didn't have time to think anything more.

"…Actually, other punishments are also possible," said Dante who, like the aged Einstein, could not hold his tongue. "Some are forbidden to smoke while working; others – for instance Balzac – aren't allowed to drink coffee, mainly not to die from consuming too much of it…"

(…while Dante is speaking, the Author will grab the chance and tell you that neither at present nor in future is he going to describe the greatness of the prairies humming in the wind; looks and individual qualities of such strange creatures as rainbow cichlids; details of the characters' clothes, ornaments of the antique furniture in their rooms, or the beauty of fuzz on their cheekbones. So Dante is dressed exactly as you imagine a man in a medieval attire.)

"…Writer's block is still a capital offence," Dante continued, "which was the sentence given to Dumas, by the way, and in order to keep him mentally healthy, other ghostwriters have been writing books for him since he arrived…"

…Pierre was in such a transitional phase of amazement when a person thinks that he is sleeping and dreaming but, at the same time, has no solid arguments to doubt the reality of what is happening. Apart from this, Hell did not look like the place that he had imagined. Moreover, some quarters in Paris (in the city where Pierre always wanted to live) and Cannes (where Pierre actually lived) resembled Hell much more than this place. Here the narrow streets were paved with pages of the books burned or torn to pieces by readers ("Sometimes the books were bad, and other times the readers were awful," Dante explained), and here and there one could see half-torn election posters as well.[9]

"The most unpleasant place is over there," Dante pointed at the corner. "It's Rue Morgue. Even professor Dowell buried his head in the sand witnessing the incredible atrocities happening there…"

"Is it a must for everyone to be condemned? I mean shall I also be sentenced to some kind of punishment?" At that moment, Pierre was pretty reluctant to move from one morgue to the other.

"Sure, it's hell. *Mea culpa*. If you wanted to live freely, you should have stayed in Cannes enjoying the

---

9 *Slaughterhouse – Five* is a well-known novel by Kurt Vonnegut, but it is unknown why the well-known book (as the Author admits) appeared in the footnote.

sunny beaches there, as your travel agencies advise. Take me, for example – if I hadn't poked my nose into the affairs of *Inferno* at one time, I wouldn't have to act as a guide for all newcomers and repeat the same dull text. True, *Repetitio est mater studiorum*,[10] but I have repeated the same words so many times that I feel like Edgar Poe's Raven."

"A very nice poem," Pierre admitted for the simple reason that Dante's speech had already spread to eight lines, and readers might have got tired of such a long monologue.

"Besides, these days everyone who makes brief sketches about a girl running a shower or an old man's foggy forehead covered with deep wrinkles, wants to become a writer and publish books… certainly, Gutenberg doesn't mind it at all – he was imprinted in the memory of posterity forever and lives in the Paradise of inventors for his great contribution to literature, while I suffer here for his stupid invention, meeting at least ten writers a day and showing them round hell… it seems, the writers will soon outnumber their readers!"

"And what's going to be my punishment?" Pierre inquired thinking of his four books and a dozen readers.

"That will be decided by Mephistopheles' Inter-Hellish Commission, but as I've told you, here writers mostly suffer for the clichés with which they tortured their readers… Something like *Divide et impera*… or whatever it is… Here, in this dark, windowless room, for example, there are locked up the writers who created the illusion of using great allusions, but in reality nothing was symbolised in their writings. Fancy

---

10 *Repetitio est mater studiorum* (Lat.) – Repetition is the mother of learning. The Author is sure that you must have heard this expression and know what it means, but still – *REPETITIO EST MATER STUDIORUM!*

that – you write something, and then the poor critics puzzle over the phrase 'lilies of the field', trying to guess whether it is an allusion from the Gospel of Matthew, or simply the phrase indicating your botanical passions."

"And what are they doing in the dark room?"

"Looking for the Cheshire cat… but the truth is…" Dante narrowed his eyes and grinned mischievously, "it's not there at all!"[11]

If only Pierre knew what punishment awaited him, he would have smiled too, but recalling his countless, sophisticated metaphors, his desire to smile died away on the way to the corner of his mouth.

"A little further, there is Sherwood Forest… plagiarists are prowling there… but you have nothing to worry about as they rob only the classic writers of their golden metaphors, brilliant similes, and valuable plots, since later they have to distribute all those among beginners and hack writers."

"You mean those poor souls, don't you?" Pierre noticed some people heading for the Sherwood Forest.

"No. They are self-recognised writers. They are destined to work hard for ever and ever to grow as many trees in the forest as were ruined to print their stupid creations."

Pierre remembered his thick books, and an unpleasant tremor ran across his back.

"I feel especially sorry for those unfortunate ones," Dante pointed to a group of people sitting by the road. "They are the writers who did not favour dialogues, and their poor readers

---

11 Ironically, an allusion of the well-known phrase of Confucius leaked in this 'allusive punishment': "It is very difficult to find a black cat in the dark room, especially if there is no black cat."

had to wait for quotation marks to appear over dozens of pages."

"Dialogues are really necessary," admitted Pierre in order to enter into dialogue with his companion. "And what are they doing there?"

Dante smiled slyly, "Waiting for Godot…"

***

"A true happy end does not exist – it's just the art of putting a full stop at the right moment."

Life is like that in a film, 2010, Pierre Sonnage

Lucy had one photographic hobby – wherever she saw reflective surfaces, she took selfies. She took them on the surface of her tea, in the car mirror, in the pupil of her friend's eye, in a shower faucet, with her iPhone in the iPhone of someone else's, in rain puddles and in a thousand other places of the kind. Most often, she took pictures instead of a shower in the bathroom and believed that with one slight movement of her finger she could seize the moment, i.e. *carpe diem*.

Lucy was a failed hipster. She always tried to erect massive barriers between herself and the masses (though she never used such old-fashioned words as "barrier" in her everyday speech; on the contrary – she tried to speak with trendy terms and buzzwords the meaning of which she herself didn't often understand). During the day, she wore glasses with coloured frames, and at night, when she took them off together with her 'hipster' mask, she became one of the statistically average girls with typical bedtime sentiments (that often seem funny in the morning) and untypical thoughts for a hipster, such as 'future is the future past' and 'past is the past future'. She was pretty, not in a sense of the word used by one's close friends as a comment for one's photo, but pretty indeed. She had long brown hair and round greenish eyes. Lucy loved writing near a TV with the sound turned down, as well as watching films (already watched three or four times) with her friends in order to see their reactions to interesting moments. She was at the age when girls still hide their diaries instead of their age. But she didn't want to be a French Frank, and the diaries – those "remnants of the Bronte era" – seemed to her too outdated in the 21st century which was much more suited to blogs. The online diaries seemed to her more comfortable, since she could write about anything in them without losing the image of a hipster or her anonymity: *"I am fond of autumn, the time when the leaves commit suicide. Oh god, why can't there be autumn all the year round?!"*

God, as a rule, did not pay attention to requests like this, but, frankly speaking, Lucy herself did not very much believe that somewhere, at the junction of the stratosphere and the mesosphere, there existed someone who could individually listen to more than six billion humans. God was a sort of placebo for her, the way of achieving her goal via belief. In addition, Lucy already had one god in the flesh on earth, too:

"Today is the presentation of Pierre's book!!! I'm waiting for it like someone waking up on Monday morning starts waiting for Friday evening!!!"

...Pierre was a writer. Maybe unknown and not even socially active, but still... Nevertheless, standing on the same platform with Houellebecq, Le Clézio, and Beigbeder wasn't easy for him. Moreover, there were only a dozen readers at the presentation of his last book...

One of them was Lucy.

Pierre and Lucy were not even close acquaintances. Theirs was the usual relationship between a writer and a reader, at the level of signing a book and pronouncing a few phrases demonstrating wit. Those witty phrases were mainly uttered by Pierre, and Lucy only smiled in response. However, at the last presentation of his book Pierre even addressed her by name. It was so unexpected she couldn't utter a word... and then Pierre made the usual witty remarks and everything went back to normal...

...A few more days will pass and Lucy, sitting under an autumn tree, will find that everything was not so simple as it seemed to her before; she will find it out while basking in the park reading page seventy-one of Pierre's new book... On it she will spot several handwritten numbers, eight words and one strange figure... It will happen exactly when Pierre enters the lift taking him up to the pinnacle of his popularity, and on the twenty-eighth floor speaks to the young girl about the individual distribution of the burden on the way to Calvary. At that very moment, Lucy will be so tired with the noise of the park and so absorbed in reading that she won't pay much attention to the silence, which will be gradually reigning around her. Such silence in books is described as ominous; as sinister as a phone call at five in the morning.

And then – Oops!

...The flight turned out to be so long that on his way to the ground Pierre first believed in Galileo's theory of falling objects, then in God, and in the end, when he approached the pavement with outstretched arms...

...The autumn leaf fell silently on the book. "One more autumnal suicide," Lucy thought and closed her book. "An ideal bookmark indeed..."

IV

Etc. & Lucy

In search of a lodging in the brave new world, Pierre had to go through hell. Baker Street turned out to be as long as the word Hippopotomonstrosesquippedalophobia,[12] and as boring as, for instance, *Buddenbrooks*. On both sides of the street there were drab rows of houses. No one was visible on the road, except for one man.

"Poor Kerouac," Dante said, "he walks and walks all day long."

Every time Pierre witnessed new punishments, he recalled

---

12 A fear of long words – phobia which the Author definitely doesn't suffer from.

his own literary sins and drenched in cold sweat as much as it was possible for someone being in hell. Otherwise, Baker Street was an ordinary street (*Via Dolorosa,*[13] as Dante put it differently) with usual advertisements ('Cheap and painless tattoo' – Larsson & co.), stencils (with Stendhal's red face on a black background), and graffiti ('Who's Afraid of Me?' – Virginia Wolf).

It was twilight time, and heavenly shades of night were falling pretty non-heavenly in Literary Hell. Only a couple of fading nimbuses flickered here and there.

"Soon Goethe's new energy project will come into effect, and there will be *more light,*"[14] Dante said about the future of Baker Street, and suddenly turned his attention to the concert poster that was glued inexpertly to the wall of a building. "Sometimes we even have fun here; especially after Kafka's arrival. He went through such a metamorphosis, you see, that it

---

13 (Lat.) A distressing or painful journey. (As you see, Dante can very well select the adequate Latin phrases when he wants to.)
14 Phrase regular for Dante and occasional for Goethe.

is impossible to recognise him: he started singing and founded a one-person band – *The Beatle*. He is still in his trial process, though…"

…However Pierre was not listening very attentively to Dante, since he thought that the insertion of 'Pierre was not listening very attentively to Dante, since he thought…' between the sentences would be as meaningless and outdated as the Hollywood effects of the last minute bomb not going off, or the police sirens at the end of the fighting scene.

"This street is mainly inhabited by the classic writers, so their punishments are also classical and individual to some extent," Dante proceeded while passing by the Royal Pet Cemetery. "Take Victor Hugo, for example, who was so scrupulous about details as we are while pronouncing the word *scrupulous* itself. So, now he sits and describes everything that was rated as *indescribable* by the writers in world literature."

Pierre was well aware that one should say nothing but good of the classic writers, since their names are as untouchable as their books on the shelves. However, he also knew that such lyrical digressions in the course of narration were as redundant as the subsequent parts of *The Three Musketeers*, and as dull as introducing similes or mere comparisons with the conjunctions *as… as* or *so… as* in every sentence…

"Poor Bulgakov is tortured over there: he writes, and writes, and writes… and, as soon as he wants to put a full stop, there appears Bradbury to burn his manuscripts…"

"But it's still Joyce who suffers worst of all – he has been forced to write footnotes for the footnotes in his books since he arrived. He has written only 10200 pages so far…"

"How long are we going to walk like this, I wonder?"

Pierre thought and started thinking about the frequent and inappropriate use of the verb 'to think' in the narrative, wishing the authors resorted to using the technology of three asterisks more often...

***

"Missing someone is not a temporal but a spatial phenomenon. Sometimes you might not have a chance to see a person for a month, and you don't mind it. But if he or she goes away and there is zero probability of encountering them, you start missing them within a week's time."

Memento Moriarty, 2008, Pierre Sonnage

Along with a hipster, Lucy was also a retrophile. As a hipster, she loved contemporary art (amorphous figures heaped together, paintings stained with colours, installations made from trash, etc.), and as a retrophile, she loved everything related to the past (except for the past perfect continuous tense, of course). Though the word 'loved', in this case, does not describe reality as precisely as the sentence 'her hipster image required her to *love*', since Godard was recognised as a god in her circle, and if we take into account her passion for Fellini, Tarkovsky and Bertolucci, we might even say that this initial monotheism had already passed into directorial polytheism...

That evening, when Lucy learnt about Pierre's free fall, she was sitting in the hall of an old cinema watching a divine comedy created by one of those deities or, to be more precise, 'something filmed by Fellini'. However, after a half-hour struggle with herself, Lucy confessed that sometimes even Fellini could be boring. Therefore, for the next half hour, she thought about how to leave the hall so that her friends would not know about her terrible cinematic blasphemy.

Fortunately, her mobile phone call came to her rescue…

It was a real tragedy amidst the comedy, she wrote in her blog later, *the worst moment in my life, an anti-fairytale which ended with 'once upon a time' …O god, how can I live further without Pierre's books?!*

God, again, was not enthusiastic to answer her; it was something like when there appears 'seen', but in reality you remain unseen. Though Pierre's deed did not go unanswered…

I hate newly-minted fans – new 'Pierreans' who have got aroused due to the PR, Lucy wrote. *They only need to know about someone's death to attack like a locust swarm! Ugh!*

But Lucy's disdain seemed as short as the weekend, for very soon she switched to decoding the cipher she had found in Pierre's new book. So, she completely forgot those worthless people – everyone who spoke about Pierre, who liked Pierre, who protected Pierre, who admired Pierre but, unfortunately for Pierre, had not even read any of his books.

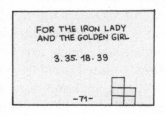

FOR THE IRON LADY
AND THE GOLDEN GIRL

3. 35. 18. 39

-71-

V

Cipher for Cipher

"Here we come," Dante said stopping in front of a high, fourteen-storey[15] building. "Shakespearean hotel 'Hothello' with perfect service, excellent rooms and efficient staff – a real paradise, so to say."

"A real paradise in hell, as they write in advertising booklets, isn't it?" Pierre smiled and immediately remembered that there were lots of more significant verbs than *smiled,* such

---

15 The Author is sure that no one will pay attention to the link between the fourteen floors of the hotel and the fourteen lines of the Shakespearean sonnet, so he has to indicate this in the footnote. Although, it should be noted that he was not at all obligated to show off with the help of such an allusion.

as *got interested,* for instance. "And how soon shall I have to grieve for the paradise lost?"

"Not before Mephistopheles' Commission decides where you have to be or not to be. But who the Hell knows, when it'll happen... so, enjoy Hell while you have time! As for me, it's high time I went back. We look forward to Vargas Llosa's arrival any minute... and since *de mortuis nil nisi bonum,* [16] I prefer to say nothing about him until I have read his books."

Pierre was never distinguished by the special love of Latin phrases. Moreover, he did not know that Dante wasn't putting profound meaning into those phrases and pronounced them in order to give the piece (or rather its footnotes) solidity. Accordingly, in response to Dante's last sentence, he nodded with the smile of someone who does not fully understand his interlocutor's words, but for some reason does not show it. As for Dante, he did not have time to think – he disappeared in the blink of an eye, without even waiting for Pierre to blink at least once, i.e. like the 25th frame effect.

The disappearance of Dante caused a punctuational tsunami in Pierre's mind – it gave rise to myriad question marks. Thinking for a while or maybe less, he took the banal decision of someone standing in front of the open doors:

He entered inside.

"Welcome to our hotel! Feel your bones at home, ha-ha..." a cheerful voice greeted him at once. "I'm here, here, sir! I want to warn you right away that I don't like it when they make fun of my appearance."

The voice was coming from the reception desk and

---

16 (Lat.) 'Of dead say nothing but good.' And as Latin is also a dead language, the Author, too, prefers to say nothing.

belonged to an ex-human being's skull who couldn't hold his tongue, even though he didn't have one.

"If this continues, I'll completely lose the ability to be surprised," Pierre thought. "Here I am, talking with a skull, and it seems to me as normal as setting an alarm clock five minutes earlier to sleep five minutes more after waking up."

"Hello, I'm Yorick, and I am a skull... ha-ha... sounds like it is in your clubs of anonymous somethings... hi, Yoooorick..." the skull greeted itself back and its eye sockets looked at Pierre. "Come and check in, sir... I've got an excellent room for you with a great view of Desdemonium... excellent room for free, one... who will pay more?... excellent room for free, two... Hey you, young man, how much would you pay for an excellent room for free? Your kingdom? Ha-ha-ha... I really like your humour. You will also like it here... Here you are, sir, take your key. Have a good rest... in peace, and don't forget to pray tonight..."

Pierre was already waiting for the lift when he heard the familiar voice again: "I can't answer the phone calls, you see... so, should you need anything, come downstairs; no need to torture yourself to death calling me, ha-ha..."

***

FOR THE IRON LADY
AND THE GOLDEN GIRL

3. 35. 18. 39

-71-

Bestseller

"...those, who don't sleep and stay up vigilant till very late at night, are their own vigilant adversaries."

Memento Moriarty, 2008, Pierre Sonnage

That night was not only absolutely sleepless but also too busy for Lucy, since it was more difficult for her to decode Pierre's cipher than Pierre himself could have probably imagined. In search of the clue, she first re-read the whole book, then looked for the 35th word on page 3, and finding the interjection 'ah' guessed that she had followed the wrong path. She even thought about Margaret Thatcher for quite a while, then recalled the legend about the daughter of King Midas, and later tried to guess the hidden meaning of the strange Tetris block drawn at the bottom of the page, but proved to be totally unsuccessful on any front in making as great a discovery as that of Schliemann's.

In general, Pierre's individual style consisted of rebuses, ciphers, riddles and other detective elements. Each of his books was such a huge action-packed lump that, as a rule, Damocles' sword over the head of the protagonist always hung on the thread of Ariadne. This was not a deduction of Sherlock Holmes, with the help of which the detective, having solved the crime very easily, still stretched investigation throughout the whole story just to make a triumphant revelatory speech only in the end. Neither was it the method of investigation by Hercule Poirot or Miss Marple, in which the identity of the criminal was revealed very soon but was carefully concealed until the last page, and in the end it turned out to be the doctor, as usual. Pierre's characters were modern detectives who thought together with the reader, and didn't wait till the last page to confess that the case was opened thanks to an accidently spotted tip of hair sticking out of the pocket of a passer-by's bag.

Therefore, Lucy's heart sensed that the clue was somewhere nearby, in every word written, but her mind did not want to enter into close relations with her heart and stubbornly rejected the game in which Pierre tried to involve her.

However, one fine day Lucy herself tried to involve Pierre in a game of her own. That day, the presentation of Pierre's third book *Life Like That in a Film* took place, and Lucy, too, tried to make her life like a film in some way. Of course, creating a new email account to send mysterious letters to the beloved writer was more like a child's banal game than a film, but Lucy believed in one simple truth: no matter how famous, busy or even arrogant a person is, he is still powerless before curiosity. So, she decided to attack Pierre's curiosity with all her lexical skills:

Dear Pierre,
You both know me and don't know me, but I know a lot about you. For instance, I know that while walking along the pavement, you always try to avoid the lines between the stones. I know that after leaving home, you come back very soon just to check if the door has been locked properly. I know that on the train you watch people with the help of their reflections in the windows of the carriage. I know that before you give a public speech, you memorise every word at night, but in front of the public you pretend to speak

*spontaneously. I know that you don't know how much
I know about you, and I also know that Socrates knew
that he knew nothing.*
*You both know me and don't know me. I am everywhere
and nowhere. I am your shadow.*
Always yours,
Lu.

P.S.
*Could you tell me why swooning is the best way
to save someone's life in books at the most critical
moments?*

And the letter worked. Firstly, because it stood out among those
few enthusiastic epistles that praised and elevated Pierre to
heaven, i.e. to the level of God; secondly, it was not like those
letters sent by beginning writers with a request to express a
good opinion about their bad stories. Moreover, it was not like
letters from indignant readers, in which Pierre's books were
referred to as a pile of papers with absolutely no literary value
("your last book is perfect – it fitted so well under the foot
of my bed that it does not wobble any more.") Leave all that
alone, Lucy's was a message urging the master of ciphers to
a fight.

A duel is always uninteresting when only one side is
fighting, so:

Dear Lu,
*If you wanted to remain anonymous, you should
have talked more about yourself, not me. Speaking of*

me, you, in fact, betrayed yourself, since people are deciphered easier than my books. You are a young girl of about twenty or twenty-two, you live in the building opposite my house, on the seventh floor, most likely. You are watching me with the help of some special equipment – I'll take a risk and say that it's binoculars. I can immediately find out your full name, but I do not want to; It's much better this way. P.S. I am also very interested in how a person who has lost consciousness can swim dozens of metres, so that in the morning he wakes up on the beach in good health.

At first, Lucy was amazed that she was deciphered so soon, then she felt even offended. Besides, Pierre's tone was too self-satisfied, something that Lucy had hated since childhood. So, she lost interest along with mysteriousness and did not answer Pierre. Neither did Pierre try hard to reassume correspondence with her. So, Lucy couldn't understand how Pierre was able to figure out her identity, especially since after this fleeting correspondence their relationship returned to the traditional form – only to the gift inscription on the book and listening to jokes invented in advance. "This cipher is probably a retribution for the unfinished game," thought Lucy, although no one (including the Author) forbade her to voice her opinion. "If life was like that in a film, I would now notice something related to the cipher. Then, because of this happy coincidence, my mind would light up, optimistic music would sound, and I would be able to solve the riddle in ten seconds… but the problem is that life is not a film."

Lucy yawned and looked at the clock. It showed 6:14, and suddenly it dawned on her:

"3:35, 18:39... it must be TIME!"

But, unlike the film, the music did not sound in her head. Moreover, exactly one minute later she realised that it was only a cliché stuck in her head thanks to the films – only a false alarm... the hands of the clock had nothing to do with iron, and even more so with gold.

"It's high time I went to bed", Lucy decided. She looked at the clock again and yawned once more to confirm her decision. "Apparently, now I can find the clue to the cipher only in my dream."

And just as she was going to stand up, a new idea struck her like Charlotte Corday:[17]

"In a dream! Gold! Iron! Lord, what a fool I am!" If she lay in a bath, she would certainly jump out of it with the words: "Eureka, Watson, Eureka! It's so elementary! E-le-men-ta-ry!"

And only then she guessed that it was not a strange Tetris block that was drawn at the bottom of the page, but the tip of Mendeleev's periodic table...[18]

**

The corridor on the third floor was completely empty.

"I love empty corridors – they are very easy to imagine,

---

17 Charlotte Corday – the murderer of Jean-Paul Marat
   Jean-Paul Marat – the victim of Charlotte Corday
18 The most honorable Mr. Mendeleev claimed that he had seen his non-elementary periodic table of elements in his dream. What fun, he had! (sceptical AN)

so there is no need to describe them in detail," Pierre thought. "Anyway, the readers always visualise their own empty corridors, so it's completely unnecessary to add such details as, for example, *the wallpaper was edged with violet colour*, or that *the doors of all rooms opened from the inside and not vice versa*."

Despite such literary indifference, Pierre soon became convinced that any word written in books was significant. He was convinced of this when he tried to enter his room but, quite unexpectedly, the door hit him directly on the nose due to the fact that it opened from the inside and not vice versa. What was more important, from an unexpected blow, he only instantly managed to see the man who ran out of the room. Hiding his face in a hood, the stranger broke into a furious gallop towards the staircase without even apologising.

In such cases, the stupidest decision is to yell at the runaway: "Hey you! Freeze, freeze!" Firstly, the person running out of all his strength will never meet this initiative with enthusiasm; and secondly, screaming, you stop dead in your tracks until you come up with the brilliant idea that if you want to stop someone, you need to chase after him.

Pierre did not think that much. He only managed to realise that if someone gallops like a horse, then he has a good reason for this, and decided to find out this reason straight from the horse's mouth. However, his pursuit turned out to be as brief as a sneeze, since as soon as Pierre approached his target, the light in the corridor went out, and the crippling darkness fell like a stone.

But as soon as Pierre was thoroughly convinced that darkness could also be hellish and even smelling of cheese, there was light. Satisfied that being in Hell he could maintain his wit and humour, Pierre looked around and realised that the situation had returned to its starting point.

The corridor on the third floor was completely empty.

***

His room proved to be so ordinary that Pierre doubted the magnificence of Shakespeare's imagination. True, he didn't quite expect to see the strangled Desdemona on the bed, but neither did such a standard atmosphere fit the standards of his expectations. The only thing associated with Shakespeare in the room was the poster over the minibar with the words: "To Beer or not to Beer."

It was clear from the very first glance that the room (with respect to the plot) had no special significance and, therefore, was categorically against occupying more than one paragraph in the narrative. Besides, the more illustrative examples there would be, the later Pierre would notice the looking-glass covered with inscriptions or the letter on the table that were waiting for him till chapter five to give rise to the whole complicated story.

Pierre again tried to recall the facial features of the runaway stranger who had left the messages for him, but soon realised that all his efforts were as meaningless as the sentences stretching out for one paragraph like this one, and he immediately switched his mind to the messages themselves.

There were two of them, but both were as obscure as the essence of the fifteen-minute closing credits at the end of Hollywood films.

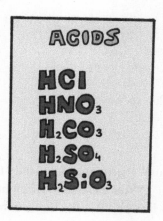

1. The inscription on the mirror contained chemicals in such quantities that Pierre's mind was poisoned, and it immediately switched to another message.

2. At first glance, the letter from the stranger seemed stranger than the question, 'Were you sleeping?' set over the

telephone at four in the morning; in other words, it was a kind of literary Babylon, in which prosaic maxims were randomly scattered.

DECANON

1) Do not write thick books. Write only what can be referred to as a good read of one-night stand.

2) Do not become a writer of only one book.

3) Learn to put a punctual full stop.

4) Read a lot and write a little – otherwise – you will write a lot but few people will read it

5) Respect your readers. Do not try to sound like a know-all.

6) Do not use ellipsis every now and then … – it is too sentimental

7) Do not kill a mocking-bird.

8) Do not plagiarize.

9) Do not use too many have-you-got-it allusions in your novel

10) Follow the above nine rules not uttering a word

"Well, well, genius!" Pierre exclaimed only to avoid repeating the verb 'thought'. "You were fond of ciphers, weren't you? So here you are – leave no Rosetta Stone unturned and find the clue to decipherment!"

In truth, Pierre had no idea why he decided that all this was a cipher. Maybe because his mind was tuned that way, or perhaps he reckoned that strangers hiding their faces under hoods would not write chemical formulae on the looking-glass for no reason...

…This was followed by three long hours, the only tangible results of which were twenty-eight balls of crumpled paper and a pen with a well-nibbled end. It proved to be more painful than Waterloo for Napoleon, more sorrowful than the last scene of 'Titanic', so Pierre's face looked more inflamed with rage than Hindenburg several minutes before the disastrous crash…

(Here the Author realises that Pierre is not able to realise anything, and realising that this is not favourable for this book, decides that Pierre must urgently meet someone more intelligent.)

…While Pierre tried to forget about his own failure with the help of historical perspectives, and the Author was having fun with simple puns, someone knocked at the door. If life was a series, then the episode two hundred and something would certainly come to an end at that very moment, but since life (and even more so the life after death) is not a series, Pierre acted as predictably as any person standing in front of the door to which they knocked.

He opened it.

Behind the door he saw the very person whom, according to the subjective opinion of the Author, Pierre needed most of all.

"Arthur Conan Doyle?!" exclaimed Pierre believing his eyes but still double-checking their guess.

"Sir… Em… Sir Arthur Ignatius Conan Doyle KStJ DL," the man corrected him with a certain pride and entered the room without asking permission. "The time has come for heavy artillery to engage in battle."

"The end of the episode two hundred and something," thought Pierre.

VI

Serial Killer

*"Never smile at a young man so that he might think
the fate is smiling upon him."*

Sphinx riddle, 2012, Pierre Sonnage

Lucy had never been fond of chemistry. True, she periodically learned some elements, but she belonged more to the category of girls who memorise the term *valency* with the help of the word 'Valentine,' consider *perm* the main achievement of chemistry, and find themselves in deep water trying to memorise what H2O stands for. At any rate, if until that day someone asked her what could be obtained by mixing lithium, bromine, argon and yttrium, she would rather get a shock than a mixture... But Pierre's cipher proved to be the only exception which (with a non-chemical mixture of chemical elements) caused at least some kind of reaction in the form of joy.

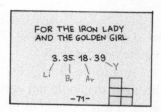

But it was a short term joy or, to be more precise, a twenty-eight-second feeling of victory, because exactly twenty-eight seconds later she guessed that: a) to find the *library* in such a huge country and b) to find *god knew what* in that library was as stupid as... um... as the desire to come up with a witty simile for "stupidity" while facing such a huge problem.

"Pierre could not be so merciless to me," Lucy reassured herself, and all of a sudden (or maybe not all of a sudden) remembered the presentation of Pierre's first book *Homo Faberge,* which was about the mystical disappearance of a Faberge egg from the museum. The presentation took place in the small hall of the *bibliothéque national de France* located in Paris. There were few visitors even then: a couple of idle readers and an old man who slept so sweetly at his desk that he couldn't be woken up.

"The first step. The first book. It is logical... Besides, there were no other libraries in our relations. A little luck and I

53

will surely find the answer to this cipher," Lucy sipped coffee from a half-full cup, and for some reason remembered Pierre's words: 'the book is also a matter of luck — reading some you lose time, while not reading others, you lose far more…'

***

"Would you like us to go to my apartment?" Claude asked the expected question quite unexpectedly.

"What are we going to do there?" the girl was eager to follow him anywhere but she could not agree immediately to his very first proposal. It was a matter of principle, after all.

"We'll see if there is something," Claude smiled and the girl guessed that this smile meant something more than just something; maybe even a couple of things.

So her principle raised a white flag, and after the announcement of ill-timed surrender, fell without a battle. Claude was a very handsome guy.

***

(While Lucy delves in the library (in vain, by the way, but she still does not know it), the Author will take the opportunity and underline that he does not at all approve of describing the places that he has never seen with his own eyes. Although since Paris is a conditional location and it does not have much significance for the story, he is not very worried about it. After all, he had already admitted that he was not going to load his narrative with all sorts of descriptions.)

The *Bibliothéque national de France* was as great as *Great Expectations*, as silent as a lamb, and as hard for the location awareness and orientation as *Middle-earth*. As for poor Lucy, she was as little as the problems of Bill Gates, as confused as *The Minds of Billy Milligan*, and as tired as Lucy herself after unsuccessful hours of searching unfamiliar clues in the familiar library hall. Though she still believed that it was better to regret what had happened than what might have happened. Therefore, she did not really regret that she had gone to the library in vain, because if she hadn't, her regrets would be stronger.

"I took the wrong path," Lucy thought as she took the train to Cannes and scrutinised the cipher again and again on her way home. "Pierre would never leave anything in a place easily reached by the others. So the clue must be somewhere else – out of the library and out of the box too…"

***

"The evening was a success… how about going to my apartment now?"

"Why such a rush on our first date…"

"Never put off until tomorrow what you could have done even yesterday."

"Oh, how sweet and well-read you are!" said the girl, shaking her golden curls and hugging Claude.

***

Lucy decided to start everything from a blank page or rather a nearly blank one, as her guess about *Library* seemed so reliable to her that even Descartes could not doubt it.

"As a rule, the answer is always in the question," Lucy thought after she stopped thinking pointlessly about the merits of Descartes for which the Author had chosen him in the previous sentence. "Maybe the library itself is the clue and not the place where it could be found; I mean, maybe I missed some detail," she decided and again opened the book on page 71. But alas! She did not find anything new there: the same final sentence of the chapter (*Labour created man and then man created everything so as not to labour any more*) and the solved rebus next to the image of the tip of Mendeleev's periodic table.

"There must be something else... longitude, latitude, address, coordinates, street, number – something that will put me on the right track," thought Lucy and immediately realised that when you try to think deeply, you can miss what is on the surface. She realised it because there was another number on that page, quite natural and organic at first glance but, apparently, it was not by chance that Pierre chose page 71 as a hint.

Lucy checked the periodic table of elements again.

"Lutetium!"

"Lu!"

***

"You know, when I see the flickering reflection of the blue screen in the dark windows, I get a feeling of comfort. That's why I like looking through the window in the evenings," the girl said.

"Yes, it's really nice. But we didn't come here to look through the window," Claude quickly drew the curtain, ruffled the girl's black hair, and smiled so strangely that the girl wanted to leave the apartment immediately, maybe even through the window...

***

Password! How couldn't she guess it so far? It was the password for the email address to which, years earlier, Lucy had sent that single letter! So Pierre did know who lived on the seventh floor of the house opposite!

Even Howard Carter was not so happy at opening the tomb of Tutankhamun as Lucy at the chance of opening Pierre's mail.

Among a lot of letters in which (if we evaluate it from a culinary point of view) 'newly-baked' fans, god only knew for what purpose, confessed their love to the deceased writer and promised him a long-term prospect of living in their hearts, there was one letter 'to Lucy'. It was so simple and so banal that Lucy stared at her name for half a minute, wondering if it contained any deep meaning. In the end she opened the mail:

> *"Hello Lucy,*
> *I'm glad you're reading this letter which means that you are cleverer than I thought. Forgive me for such frankness, but I am already dead and the dead are forgiven for everything except for establishing concentration camps and killing half of humanity.*
> *Not quite for the first time, but probably for the billion*

and a hundred millionth time there was a word and the word was 'voyeurism'. I agree that saying the word and rejoicing that you are aware of its meaning is mere snobbery. But if you don't know this word, I'll explain that it means to spy on someone else's life for a certain purpose. You're not a typical voyeurist, but probably it's not all alien to you. This is exactly what betrayed you. Actually, it was very easy to guess who you were: in your letter I found such details that you would not have known about me just running after me through the streets – you must have seen me at home. Besides, on one-time observation, no conclusions are drawn; permanent observation is needed. Based on this, I guessed that you lived on the opposite side of the street. Our buildings are not quite close, which meant that you needed some kind of device for observation, for example binoculars. The style of your letter made me think that you were probably much younger than me, and had got carried away by creating a romantic fog. Accordingly, there formed an image of a young girl living on the opposite side of the street who read my books and liked me, or who liked me and read my books. Everything was extremely clear except your exact location. This was also not difficult to calculate: you had sent a letter with your conclusions about me and, naturally, you would be interested in my reaction. Consequently, it was very likely that you would try to observe me reading your letter; in fact, I was absolutely sure that you would. Realising all this, I immediately looked out. You were afraid that

I would spot you and urgently moved away from the window. The curtain flapped and I noticed it. For verification purposes, I wrote a response letter and sent it. You did not answer, which meant that I was right. Voilà! Finita la commedia.

However, I am not writing this letter in order to boast of my not quite extraordinary abilities, especially since now I am dead and I no longer need to. I just want to share a story, since you really deserve it. I wrote it for you, and it is a matter of life and death for you, so to say...”

The story in the form of a document was attached to the letter, and Lucy opened it as well:

“Sundays were days-off for Claude. On those days he killed no one but time and chose the next victim...”

VII

Conan's Canon

Pierre had been fond of Sherlock Holmes since childhood. True, he never understood how one could find out with the help of a speck on the nail of the ring finger of somebody's right hand that two days earlier, at 2 a.m. sharp, he or she was making papaya preserve on the third floor of the house inherited from an uncle, and that a dog was running around in the room right at that moment. Nevertheless, Pierre realised that he loved the Baker Street detective just because he never understood.

He himself took more after Moriarty who managed to complicate situations easier than unravel them. But when he saw the literary father of the two characters next to him, he felt as helpless and miserable as Gulliver would if he found himself in New York straight after the Lilliput Island.

Before discussing the letter, Conan Doyle carefully studied the inscription on the looking-glass and came to two conclusions: first – those were the formulae of hydrochloric, nitric, carbonic, sulfuric, and silicic acids; second – yes, those were the formulae of hydrochloric, nitric, carbonic, sulfuric, and silicic acids, but so what? And he turned all his attention to the letter.

"The lines are interesting, but we have to read between them," Pierre said in such an uncertain tone with which one shouldn't speak at an interview if one wants to convince the employer of something.

"Be a little more confident," Conan Doyle seemed so surprised at Pierre's shyness, as if he himself had to solve complicated cases together with his beloved writer every day. "What do you think about this letter?"

DECANON

1) Do not write thick books. Write only what can be referred to as a good read of one-night stand.

2) Do not become a writer of only one book.

3) Learn to put a punctual full stop.

4) Read a lot and write a little – otherwise – you will write a lot but few people will read it

5) Respect your readers. Do not try to sound like a know-all.

6) Do not use ellipsis every now and then ... – it is too sentimental

7) Do not kill a mocking-bird.

8) Do not plagiarize.

Bestseller

9) Do not use too many have-you-got-it allusions in your novel

10) Follow the above nine rules not uttering a word

Pierre thought that it was a real shame even to think that he thought nothing, and with a thoughtful look, pretending to be fully competent, replied that he was still thinking about it.

"Well, let's start at the beginning. First of all, welcome to the Detective Club," said Conan Doyle and nodded his head in greeting. "We have only two rules here: rule number one – no rules at all; rule number two – all rules have exceptions, including the first one."

Generally, Pierre was good at logic, but now not only the letter, but also the rules of the Detective Club puzzled him.

"As a rule," said Conan Doyle and paused emphasising the situational irony of starting the new sentence with the third rule after underlying the possibility of only two, "when there is no other way out, we should try to find something unusual, for instance the unusual use of dashes in this letter. I want to say that here the author of these sentences must have chosen the incorrect variants correctly; that is to say, he has deliberately chosen the incorrect variant for some particular reason. Besides…"

(While Pierre and Conan Doyle are discussing the messages [or rather, only Conan Doyle is discussing them and Pierre is listening to him], the Author will traditionally take a break and express his worries about Pierre as a character, since the latter has not yet revealed specific characteristics of his nature and,

therefore, it is difficult for him to become memorable for the reader. So, the Author decides to radically change him by removing his loser complex and, before it is too late, make him more self-confident and sarcastic.)

"Wait a minute, my dear Arthur," Pierre sounded sarcastic, "I'm not Dr. Watson, who only admires Sherlock Holmes' intuition and insight, and who is asked for an opinion only when everything is already clear…"

Sir Arthur seemed puzzled. In his last statement Pierre said a lot more words than he had uttered so far.

"You suggest to start at the beginning, but I prefer to start at the very end," Pierre continued, and so that his words would not sound like a pun or a bad joke, he added: "I mean the tenth paragraph which suggests…"

"But first, let me explain everything briefly and clearly," Conan Doyle interrupted him and just in case, even coughed.

Pierre knew that, as a rule, any introduction beginning with the words 'let me explain everything briefly and clearly' was a prerequisite for a sophisticated and incomprehensible speech. Nevertheless, he listened to Conan Doyle with patience.

"I love puzzles, I love deduction, I like to investigate, but I'm not Sherlock Holmes; I mean, this letter is by no means an open book for me; even if it were, what is the point of an open book if you are illiterate? Therefore, I now feel like an archaeologist who has found a jaw bone that doesn't belong to any *Homo*. So, if we can't solve this riddle by joint forces, I'll definitely freak out."

Pierre smiled. Even the fantastic Mr. Doyle asked

him for help.

"If humans shot bullets as often as they shoot words, then life would have long ceased on earth," said Pierre who had no idea when he had become so sarcastic. "I agree with your assumption that the author of this letter might not be very good at the rules of punctuation, but sometimes it's not at all necessary to know those rules in order to come to a full stop."

"So put it!" Conan Doyle looked at Pierre with such suspicion as if he were an expired product on the counter.

"Punctuation marks have been misused in places, but they are put exactly where they ought to be," inhaled Pierre. "So here completely different things must be out of place, and in order to guess it you just need to take into account the last instruction – "Follow the above nine rules… *not uttering a word*.""

"That is?"

"That is," exhaled Pierre, "we should behave contrary to Hamlet."

"That is?"

"That is… that is… if you are asked, you are crazy about Shakespeare," grumbled Pierre. "I mean we should ignore the words… words… words…"

"What should we read then, only punctuation marks, or what?"

"Maybe full stops and dashes, individually, are punctuation marks, but together they make up the Morse code alphabet consisting of dots and dashes. Based on this, the first nine sentences are nothing but nine letters of one word, it's elementary, Sir!"

*(Here, the Author notes that complacency is also
suitable for such a sarcastic attitude and decides that
it would be good to introduce this touch, too, into the
protagonist's character.)*

"There was a time when I knew this alphabet by heart," Pierre
said with some complacency, "but then I realised that one
shouldn't litter one's mind with all kinds of rubbish when
there is the greatest informative garbage dump in the world...
by the way, is Wi-Fi available in this hotel?"

*(Describing the hotel room, the Author forgot to say
that each room was equipped with a computer of the
same company – MEPHISTAPPLE.)*

"Jules Verne was going to internetise Literary Hell," Conan
Doyle shrugged, "but Mephistopheles did not allow him,
saying that it was impossible to come up with a more horrible
Hell than living without the Internet."

Pierre knew that it was never too late to give up some
idea, and before doing that, he tried to find a different solution
to the problem:

"Why can't we get the Wi-Fi of paradise?"

"We can, but we don't know the password," Conan Doyle
answered trying to convince Pierre that they were in a blind
alley with no way out.

The silence was crowned in the room, and it already
reigned all around.

"Don't worry, when it comes to passwords, I take to them
like a duck takes to water," Pierre replied with a smug look,

citing a trite and outdated simile. "In Hollywood films, people tend to choose the names of their children as passwords. So, let's try 'Jesus'…"

***

"Sundays were days off for Claude. On those days he killed no one but time and chose the next victim. He killed time without a special motive, probably just to kill his unbridled passion for killing, the reason of which was unknown; at any rate, psychologists or other people with a profession containing the element 'psycho' in its name could not claim that this was due to a childhood trauma, since the family where he grew up was as happy as all the other happy families.

He was a good-looking young man; good-looking in the sense of the word each girl would invest in it according to their own taste. Therefore, enchanted female representatives easily fell into his trap, especially when he promised them magic circumstances. And he was right in a way, since many entered his apartment, but scarcely anyone came back from there.

For neighbours, Claude was a decent young man. True, this impression was not justified by anything other than the fact that noise was never heard from his apartment, and he never flooded the lower floors, but still.

The girls went up to his apartment standing on their own feet, and later Claude carried them out of

*there with his own hands. No one knew how Claude
managed to go unnoticed, while on the seventh floor
of the house on the opposite side there lived a very
curious girl..."*

Lucy stopped reading. This was no longer a childish game
with chemical elements. The storyline led to the conclusion
that the next victim would be Lucy herself. True, she was not
acquainted with Claude, she had not noticed anything strange
about him while watching Pierre, and all this story was pure
fantasy, but still. "Well, life is not a book, of course, but it can
be described in a book," she assumed and continued reading
with such a sinister feeling which occurs to a person in the
short time interval between a flash of lightning and the sound
of thunder.

*Claude had no idea that the window represented
a grave danger to him; that it looked like a small,
flickering blue monitor that periodically displayed
life dramas. Neither did he know that in order to
penetrate through the window it was not necessary
to have a propeller on your back or a web shooter
on your wrist; that sometimes even binoculars were
sufficient for that. Those binoculars in the hands of
the girl living on the seventh floor of the house on
the opposite side posed a greater danger for Claude
than the death of Bruce Willis would for the earth just
before Armageddon.*

*As for the girl from the seventh floor, she lived
completely carefree until the day she discovered the*

numbers, letters, and a strange pattern in her newly-bought book..."

At this point the narrative stopped (not because Pierre had forgotten to write further, but because he could not write about the things that had not happened yet) and Lucy realised that it was her who had to finish the story.

***

True, Pierre took to passwords like a duck takes to water, but soon he discovered that his water was poured into an aquarium. He discovered it having tried 'Stairway', 'Let there be internet', 'knockknockknockin' and many other versions, but alas – all his efforts were in vain. He sought but could not find, he asked but was not given, he knocked but the door was not opened to him...

"When Sherlock Holmes comes to a standstill, he always starts to think about what he would do if he were a criminal..." Conan Doyle began and instantly realised that over the past few suggestions, his only function seemed to be maintaining a dialogue.

"If it were up to me, I would demand that only the logically calculated passwords be set on the Internet," smiled Pierre, "life would be much more interesting that way. For instance, if I were asked to select the password for paradise, I'd come up with something connected with the essence of password cracking."

And suddenly his mind brightened...

(Here the Author is worried that he had to use such a hackneyed phrase as 'his mind brightened', but he

justifies himself by the fact that Pierre could not figure out the right password, while the Author had no spare lines to spend on Pierre's endless philosophising.)

"You have guessed something, haven't you?"

"I guessed what I would choose if I were in their shoes!" said Pierre, enjoying his discernment, *"thou shalt not steal!"*

So they tried it and... stole.

***

Lucy did not like crowded places. Accordingly, she loved the presentations of books. She was especially fond of unknown writers – those who were surprised to see more than three unfamiliar people at their own presentations. And there were many of them. Many wrote, and many wanted to have a book as an indisputable proof of being a writer... or, more often, not being a writer at all.

Pierre was an exception; he was unknown but his books were not so bad, though standing on the same platform with Houellebecq, Le Clézio, and Beigbeder still wasn't easy for him. Moreover, there were only a dozen readers at the presentation of his last book...

...and one of them was Claude.

But Claude paid little attention to Pierre; he was scrutinising the first row where a beautiful girl with brown hair was sitting and waiting impatiently to get the Author's autograph on her new book.

The cat-and-mouse game has begun...

***

~~~
1) .-.   2) .    3) .
4) --    5) .-.  6) ...-
7) -.    8) .    9) ---
~~~

...There was dead silence in the room. The two other dead – Conan Doyle and Pierre – were as quiet as a computer mouse while converting punctuation marks into letters.

(Here the Author is glad that there is no clock in the room, and he does not have to write nonsense like 'only the ticking of the clock broke the dead silence'.)

In principle, after the principle was found, decoding the message did not take much time:

~~~
1) R   2) E   3) E
4) M   5) R   6) V
7) N   8) E   9) O
~~~

"That's it!" Conan Doyle put the sheet of paper on the table and stared at the letters. "I think it won't be difficult to make up the word now."

"I'm still thinking about those acids," Pierre glanced back to where 'ACIDS' was written in capital letters.

"You need to follow the second track only after the first

is totally lost."

"All right," agreed Pierre and went back to the letters: "EVEN ROME, EVEN MORE, EVER ENORM…"

Conan Doyle shook his head like the teacher who is unhappy with the student's response, but does not want to spoil his mood.

"OVER REMEN, REMOVE REN, EVEN ROME…"

"Let's keep silent for a while," Conan Doyle suggested, "because you are already repeating one and the same text."

"I'm repeating one and the same text…" Pierre remembered Dante Alighieri complaining about the same and suddenly his mind brightened again:

"NEVERMORE!"

VIII

Out of the Box

Edgar Allan Poe lived at N 13 Rue Morgue together with a
black cat, black raven, and black humour. He had only two
dreams: 1st – he wanted each person's dream always to come
true, and 2nd – he wanted his 1st dream never to come true. In
the mornings he trained his cat in being an omen of misfortune,
and in the evenings he wrote soul-destroying stories to get
destroyed souls cheaply and, through Gogol's mediation,
resell them at good price to Mephistopheles.

Poe rarely left the house – only once a year – and received
guests even more rarely – never. Therefore, the fact that he
invited some writers to his place on the one hundred and sixty-

fifth anniversary of his death[19] aroused widespread surprise.

Rue Morgue in Literary Hell was on the list of unfavourable places. There was a constant polar night there, and along with the traditional hooting of an owl, there sounded the same kind of sinister music as in horror films when the main character enters an unfamiliar house.

Accordingly, it was very strange that Rue Morgue was unusually peaceful that day. Neither the invited writers fell victim to the street attacks nor did anything fell on their heads from the windows. Their peaceful arrival to Poe's house with the inscription HELLCOME above the doorway, seemed uneasily embarrassing and amazing...

...However, as the guests found out later, it was not the only thing that would amaze them that day.

***

Extract from the interrogation conducted by Conan Doyle:

Orwell: The door opened on its own accord. It was dark in the room. Only one candle was burning on the table. There was nobody around, but I felt as though someone was watching us.

Hugo: We sat at the table. Only empty plates and forks were lying before us. I don't know exactly what happened next, but I would like to draw your attention to the floral ornament of those forks. It was an unknown flower on the pistil of which one could see the whole spectrum of yellow particles, and its stamens, due to their microsporangia, looked

---

19 The day of one's death is the equivalent of one's birthday in Hell, and the dead celebrate it as the day of their otherworldly birth (erudite A/N).

amazingly natural. I would also note the head of the forks, six sharp points of which resembled bayonets... as if it were a group of rebellious peasants during the French Revolution... As for the handles...

Beckett: Then we waited for the host but he didn't come.

Orwell: Suddenly I was overcome by animal fear. A man in a hood came out of the darkness.

Oscar Wilde: I can swear it wasn't Poe... Damn, such an ordinary sentence. I have to be smarter. Just a moment...

Milton: I can't remember the details, since I found myself in a dark darkness.

Wells: He looked like a Martian... or like a time traveller created by synthesising dinosaur DNA and euglena viridis proteins in a test tube...

Joyce: He smiled a crescent-smile... By the way, this phrase is an allusion to the line of the poem by an unknown Irish poet Damian O'Someone in which the author, in his turn, reveals the influence of a magnificent ornithologist from Costa Rica... Em... no, no... well, what I was talking about?... Ah yes, so he smiled and put on the table a black box similar to Malevich's Black Square but only in a spatial dimension, which, in its turn, reminded me of one episode from the *Epic of Gilgamesh*: "When Enkidu noticed a totally different dimension in the space..." Ah yes, speaking about Enkidu, I remember...

Beckett: We were not going to ask him, "Who are you?" But neither were we going to say that we were not going to ask him, "Who are you?" ...So we asked him who he was.

Joyce: By the way, Byron's poems...

Hugo: I noticed a narrow scar on his forehead. It looked

like the strait between Scylla and Charybdis…

Orwell: Sure, we are not swine, but they could have put something to eat on the table… these people have completely lost their humanity…

Oscar Wilde: When people tell you that everything will be all right, ask them 'when?'… um… as I did when he said that Poe had disappeared in obscure circumstances, and he really regretted that we had been disturbed in vain…

Beckett: I asked him: "Where is Poe?" and he answered: "Nowhere." "When will he come?" I asked again. "Yesterday," he answered.

Wells:… And suddenly he disappeared…

Milton: in the blink of an… er… ear.

Joyce: Where did I stop? Wait a minute, I'll start at the beginning and recall… Yes, he smiled a crescent-smile…

Hugo: Then the door opened. It was made of oak, with magnificent hinges, one and a half metres wide by three metres high, a little rough, with a round handle and an excellent lock… And then you entered…

Wells: In my opinion, the key to secret is in the black box.

***

"To feel the excitement of travelling with the help of Google Earth is the same as to be sated by reading cook books."

Homo Faberge, 2006, Pierre Sonnage

Lucy was a *filmosopher.* She loved the films where there was invested more sense than money. However, she watched films of all genres – those that she liked and those that she 'ought to like' (the Art house films, for example). As a filmosopher, she believed that in every film there was some sort of meaning (even in those in which a couple is doomed to fall in love with each other, and their love affair lasts an hour and a half only for the purpose of admitting – puffing and perspiring heavily, right at the altar or at the plane's steps – that he or she is an idiot...)

...And since Lucy saw so many films that she tried to behave exactly like the film characters, she decided not to say anything to the police. Firstly, because the police would have come only when everything had already happened, and secondly, she had no evidence against Claude. She could not tell them that one suicide writer left her a story about a maniac, and they had to arrest the guy with whom she wasn't even acquainted. Even if they caught him when he led the girl to his place, did the guys take the girls to their apartments just to kill them?

As for Claude, she found him very easily, since he lived right opposite. In the evenings, Lucy sat by the window as a spectator in the theatre and waited for the curtain to rise in the literal and figurative sense. Claude, basically, was alone and wrote something all the time ('probably a diary where he describes his manic thoughts...') Several times she noticed him with different girls. However, against all theatrical laws, he declared an intermission and lowered the curtain just at the moment when the tragedy was to break out. Therefore, Lucy did not see anything suspicious. Naturally, she did not expect to see windows stained with blood or a sack thrown out of the apartment with a corpse cut to pieces, but Claude lived an unusually usual and boring life for a serial killer.

Because of this, a few days later, Lucy realised that her observation was gradually moving from the genre of horror films to that of the everyday-life films, and this time she decided to get into the act herself.

***

Pierre was interested in three things: 1st – Why his punishment was late; 2nd – Who was that stranger, and 3rd – Why the Author decided that he was interested in three things when actually he was interested in only two.

As for Conan Doyle, he was not at all interested in what Pierre was interested in. He carefully studied the objects that had been taken out of a box left by the stranger:

- a small picture of a grey square
- two clocks: one – stopped, the other – without hands
- a bitten apple
- *The Odyssey* by Homer
- an ordinary joker card.

"I will soon develop an allergy to all these puzzles," said Pierre, picking up the picture and thinking how the Author couldn't get bored commenting on his actions. "Have you got any solution?"

"Before getting to answers, you should first put the questions," said Conan Doyle with the same wise air characteristic of people who use the words 'arrogant', 'scepticism', and 'substantial' in one sentence. "For example, I wonder why it was necessary to gather all those writers, while our friend, the stranger, could have passed all these items to us through Poe…"

(Here the Author suspects that Conan Doyle and Pierre will not finish the tedious discussion soon, and in order not to let the reader get bored, he will try to recall some interesting facts from Pierre's life; For instance, the fact that he never understands the essence of taking photos, because every photo for him is only "the conserved melancholy, which may reveal itself years later." Or the fact that Pierre always calls the phone numbers that film characters dictate to someone, as well as the fact that he, sitting in a café, likes to watch strangers or a couple, and make deductive conclusions about them, but can

*never check the validity of his guesses, since he is too
shy to check their accuracy. Or, even... Ah, well, here
we go again...)*

"...i.e. we concluded that the guests and the objects were
not selected at random, and there is some kind of connection
between them," Conan Doyle summarised the discussion.

"In other words, we have seven writers and six objects."
Pierre made two lists:

1. GEORGE ORWELL	1. A SMALL PICTURE
2. JOHN MILTON	2. A BITTEN APPLE
3. VICTOR HUGO	3. A CLOCK WITHOUT HANDS
4. OSCAR WILDE	4. A JOKER CARD
5. HERBERT WELLS	5. THE "ODYSSEY"
6. SAMUEL BECKET	6. A STOPPED CLOCK - 7:48
7. JAMES JOYCE	

*(According to the Author, it's high time that, if not
Pierre, then at least Conan Doyle guessed that the
works of the above-mentioned authors are encrypted
in the objects. Otherwise, it will be very embarrassing,
because everyone has already guessed it.)*

"I think, we need to use little grey cells better to see the whole
picture..." Pierre picked up the grey picture again, and the
Author can no longer count how many times again he will
have to say (for the third time – A/N) that Pierre's mind
brightened. "Wait a minute! Grey... picture... *The Picture of
Dorian Gray!*"

"i.e. the works of the authors are encrypted in these objects…" Conan Doyle proved to be very good at summarising the discussions.

"Aaand the Oscar goes… home," Pierre smiled and instantly realised that Conan Doyle would not be able to get his joke.

"And Joyce, too," Conan Doyle put *The Odyssey* aside, and to make his action argumentative, he added: *"Ulysses!"*

"This apple will be associated with Milton," Pierre said with a greedy expression and, like Adam, took a second bite from the already bitten apple. *Paradise Lost.*

"Hmm… the clocks will be more difficult," Conan Doyle took one of them and looked closely at it. "This one belongs to a drunkard who doesn't suffer from constipation; he has two eyes, sleeps at night, breathes… Oh, I beg your pardon! I got carried away…"

"Personally, I can't recall anything with the word clock in its title," said Pierre and for the first time felt sorry that he liked writing novels more than reading them.

"Maybe it's not the clock but the time that matters here – 7:48… Does it remind you of anything?"

"*Voila!* Not seven but nineteen; 19:48! Orwell, *1984*. He finished the book in 1948, and according to one version, he simply replaced the numbers to get the title," Pierre expressed his general education and saved the Author from another use of footnotes.

"Then the other clock is Beckett," Conan Doyle smiled, and then smiled again realising how often he smiled. "It must be Beckett for two reasons: 1st – the clock without hands shows indefinite time, and indefinite time means endless waiting which, in its turn, is associated with *Waiting for Godot*…"

"And what's the second reason?"

"The second reason is that I have never heard of Beckett's other works."

The logic was iron, like an iron curtain.

"Strange. Only two writers are left, and a joker, who makes people laugh," Conan Doyle looked at the playing card.

"Consequently, he himself laughs as well. Au revoir, Victor! VIVA LA VICTORIA!" Pierre proudly crossed his legs (as the Author was bored of writing 'said', 'smiled', or 'shrugged'). "The task was not difficult at all. So, let's call Herbert Wells, and the rest can leave now."

***

> *"There are two types of people in the world,*
> *those who divide people into two types,*
> *and those who do not."*

Jeremy Bentham

Only three things seemed more boring to Lucy than waiting: watching a chess championship, sitting at home on Friday evenings, and conducting permanent sociological polls. In general, if it were up to her, she would conduct one single sociological study on whether it was necessary to conduct such studies at all. Despite this, she decided to conduct a sociological study rather than wait, since sociologists had one privilege – they were trusted and easily allowed into the house even when the house belonged to a serial killer…

…the glass peephole on the door reflected Lucy, so she first took a selfie and only then knocked on the door. She felt the knife in her pocket. She did not have plan A or plan B, not to mention the rest of the letters of the alphabet. In films there was always some way out in dangerous situations, so she was sure that this time there would be some way out as well.

She knocked again.

"Hope I won't have to knock on another door soon," she thought, "for example, on heaven's door."

("Claude!" No answer." Claude!" No answer.)

No one opened the door. So Lucy pushed it and realised that there was no need to open it: "Hello, is anyone there?" she shouted just in case (and for decency, of course). The apartment was silent. She carefully walked down the corridor. "He might be sleeping… I'll check his writing and leave right away." Earlier she always wondered why the film characters entered the house where, with a high probability, someone close to a monster lived. "Curiosity has bigger eyes than fear," she concluded when she found herself in the familiar room which was lit better than the rest of the apartment. The familiar window, familiar table, familiar surroundings… On the table there were spread some sheets, so she read one of them:

"Pierre Sonnage told me that when I am not able to write anything, I should write about how I can't write. So I write, or rather cannot write. But there are so many things that I would like to write about; take that girl living in the appartment opposite, for instance…"

The sound of tiptoeing was heard from the corridor.

(The Author knows that 'sound of tiptoeing' sounds odd, but 'deadly silence was broken' would sound too sinister.)

"Who's there?" Lucy forgot that she was in someone else's apartment.

Time stopped for a while, but then Claude entered the room (or, to be more precise, he appeared in the doorway) and smiled at the girl:

"Hello, Lucy! I was expecting you."

***

Pierre guessed that they were deadlocked. Herbert Wells not only had no idea about all this but also about why he should.

"In my opinion, there is some sort of mistake here," he was even too lazy to shrug, "no one gave me any clues… or maybe they did, but I forgot them when the aliens kidnapped me, washed out my brains and returned me as a completely different person… Actually, my real 'self' is now on another planet, and he will come back here only in case he wants to unmask me, and if my other 'self', who was born two centuries earlier than me and is now travelling in parallel reality will be able to…"

"What a curse! His fantastic retreats are already… Come back to reality, damn it!" The author of *The Lost World* interrupted him. "Maybe we made a mistake and attributed some object to another author?"

"Maybe yes and maybe no. Who knows…" Wells said, "perhaps there was some object in this box, but for some reason it disappeared into the black hole between the worlds; but I have nothing to do with it."

"Why?" Pierre posed a universal question for those cases when a person does not know what to ask.

"Wells has nothing to do with it, that's why," Conan Doyle answered for Wells. "The box is empty; at any rate, nothing more is seen inside there... Doesn't it remind you of anything from his novels? Yes! *The Invisible Man!* Seven writers and seven associations, that's it! We came to the end."

"Never mind, anyway we are all going to die," this time Wells shrugged and for more variety, he even pushed out his lower lip. "Then the aliens will take us away and brainwash us to create a new race – Aliens Alliance..."

"Oh, boy! Now I'll take this box and smash his head with it!" Pierre suddenly showed such a reaction which was inappropriate not only for a refined character in a book, but also for a statistically average polite person.

"The box... the box!" Conan Doyle exclaimed and this time it was his turn to brighten: "We have excluded the objects and forgot all about the box in which they were. The main clue is the box!"

(At this point, if it were up to the Author, there would be an exciting piece of music)

"But have we got the writer whose secret could be kept in a black box?"

And before Herbert Wells began to lecture on the works of some writers from the future and their bad influence, Pierre took the floor and answered so casually, as if he had been thinking about this issue all his life: "Antoine de Saint-Exupéry…"[20]

---

20 Here the Author wants to remind himself that the black box – a flight recorder in an aircraft – is actually orange in colour.

IX

The Anonymous Suicide Club

Our life begins banally, as a rule: we are born, and once born, grow. In other words, we are all products of our childhood and head along the roads that we take or, more often, are forced to take. Then we live or exist until it comes to the full stop which then transforms (or we transform it after our own free will) into a dash between two dates…

…The Anonymous Suicide Club in Literary Hell was as trendy as, for instance, senseless Hashtags or taking pictures of illusory kisses at the Great Sphinx of Giza. The club members were the writers who had committed suicide secretly, without warning the world, and their death was considered to be natural. The club was chaired by Albert Camus who avoided strangers like the plague. Therefore, the only condition for those who wanted to join was to be anonymous suicides. Club members gathered on Sundays, when the rest of the writers had a day off and rested from their punishment. On this day, some slept like the dead, and some others were referred to as 'lazybones' for their laziness. However, the members of the club were far from lazy, and on Sundays they worked till dead of night to develop their club further.

"We live to die," Camus would repeat the club slogan lifelessly. "It is absurd to start reading a book whose end you know in advance, absurd! What is our life? Only templates in the biography that need to be completed gradually in order to grow old and die some day, or to die so as not to grow old. How boring! You plan a car accident, commit suicide, and they interpret it primitively: *Ironically, the writer Albert Camus, who was an absurdist philosopher and wrote about the absurdity*[21]...blah blah blah..."

Antoine de Saint-Exupéry was a club member with considerable experience. He had joined it the moment he followed in his character's footsteps and to commit suicide, he stopped controlling the plane in the air...

...For that he was now constantly floating around the club, having no other punishment or anything else to do. *This man has such a kind soul that it will suffer witnessing the sufferings of others*, *HE* had decided in this way, it seemed.

---

21 According to official information, Albert Camus really died in a car accident. But in his pocket was found an unused ticket for the train heading in the same direction, which gave journalists the opportunity to emphasise the absurdity of this case (official A/N).

Bestseller

The suicides gathered in the club, talked about their concerns and thus calmed their slain selves. Occasionally they even discussed some issues, such as, for instance, 'Suicide as a Mainstream,' the presenter of which was going to be the very Antoine de Saint-Exupéry that day. The title of the presentation was chosen very successfully. Firstly, because any topic in the title of which the word "mainstream" is used creates an illusion of being interesting; and secondly, because everyone likes to make fun of the mainstream so that they themselves seem better.

That day the anonymous suicides were expecting a new member at the meeting.

***

"Hello, I'm Alexandr Sergeevich Pushkin. When you die young, they praise you more. Therefore, I intentionally planned a duel. I am an anonymous suicide."

"Hello, I'm Agatha Christie. I, too, am a… what's the word… Well, I am whatever it is… But I forgot why."

"Hello, I am not a writer. But before setting fire to the house, I wrote such a wonderful farewell letter that I ended up in Literary Hell. Unfortunately, that letter burned with me, so I'm an anonymous suicide."

"Hello, I'm Jerome Salinger. When I committed suicide due to boredom, people only later realised that I was still alive. I am an anonymous suicide…"

The ritual, traditionally, went counterclockwise and, from time to time, there sounded such a loud and polyphonic 'Hel-loooo' in response that it would even wake up a dead man in his grave.

"Hello, I am Pierre Sonagge, a newcomer. I decided to commit suicide in order to become popular. But since I didn't leave a letter or say anything to anyone, the journalists decided that I was a victim of an accident. Therefore, I'm also considered an anonymous suicide so far…"

"Hel-looo, Pieeeer…"

***

"Hello, Claude," Lucy greeted him back and began recalling the best moments of her short happy life as she didn't want to miss anything important when her life would flash before her eyes.

There was nowhere to escape; neither was there any reason for that so far.

"Have you read them?" Claude asked her pointing to the papers scattered on the table. But Lucy was only able to read what was written on his forehead – nothing promising or soothing.

"If I say 'yes', he will kill me right away, and if I say 'no', he'll do it a bit later," Lucy thought, and she answered exactly as the failed sociologist would:

"Hard to answer."

Claude laughed.

"You are too tense, relax a bit; I'm not going to eat you…"

"So that's what happens with the corpses," Lucy thought, "he gobbles them up!"

(Here the Author thinks that Lucy is exaggerating

– she shouldn't have watched The Silence of the Lambs.*)*

"Now take a seat and read," Claude pointed to the chair. "Who knows, perhaps you'll be able to explain it all."

Lucy had always wondered why the killers were telling their victims about their unhappy childhood, and why they were talking about the vanity of life until someone showed up and shot them directly in the head. But now she realised that she, too, was in exactly the same situation. Then she thought it would be nice if tears appeared in Claude's eyes, as she would be able to take a selfie in them. But she did her best to overcome her craving for selfies, sat at the table and began to read…

***

"Who can tell me what is depicted in this picture?" de Saint-Exupéry pointed to a hat-shaped silhouette.

"Boa constr…" Pierre, like anyone else, loved to show his knowledge, but he was interrupted.

"Hush, we know that you know," said Camus, "everyone knows that everyone knows, but he is so happy to hear *a hat* in response that we try not to break his heart."

And then he said aloud: "A hat, of course!"

"Of course!" de Saint-Exupéry replied joyfully. "I knew it! Everyone says that! You, grown-ups, are so strange – you work yourselves to death and don't remember that you were once children! I committed suicide because I couldn't live in such a world... the world where filmstars are appreciated more than the stars in the sky; the world where they kill their dreams more often than the lights at night; the world where they whitewash the ceilings stained with rain water rather than try to see different silhouettes in those wonderful stains; the world where they fight for peace in vain, and where they are too lazy to live in peace; the world where the nature is treated unnaturally, and where the problems of animals are shouldered only when a certain Coco Chanel introduces natural furs in the new collection of the year... Yes, I don't like the world where princes hunt foxes, and where pragmatists consider idealists crazy... I was ashamed to live in such a world and that was why I committed suicide. But now I am embarrassed because in the same world even suicide has lost its value..."

"It has already reached the point where death is the main factor in acknowledging a piece of literature..." murmured Camus.

"It has already reached the point where death is the main factor in acknowledging a piece of literature, and the work is considered more dramatic if the cause of the death is suicide. On the other hand, the era of Madam Bovary and Anna Karenina has passed. At present other climaxes are needed, for it's very easy to kill. You make the reader get fond of the characters and then – bang-bang – you kill them to create the impression of something deep… existential…"

"How did you know in advance what he would say?" Pierre got so sincerely interested in the matter that the Author decided to start the sentence with the phrase, 'Pierre got so sincerely interested in the matter…'

"He repeats this text every now and then. When his plane crashed, he hit his head badly and has been having memory problems since. We are hearing all this for the forty-fourth time now…"

"I hate numbers, and I don't trust statistics because statistically every other statistic is erroneous. Besides, so many writers kill their characters for tragic effect that I've lost count. Therefore, I am wholeheartedly beseeching you not to kill them, because this way you are killing not only *them* but also the readers' *interest*, and it will result in the death of *literature* as such…"

"Thank you," someone sitting next to Pierre whispered.

"Thank you!" de Saint-Exupéry lowered his head expecting applause. And there came such deafening applause that one might think one was at a Beethoven concert.

***

"Pierre Sonnage told me that when I am not able to write anything, I should write about how I can't write. So I write, or rather cannot write. But there are so many things I would like to write about; take that girl living opposite, for instance…

Her name is Lucy. However, her idea about me is the same as about the Wabi-Sabi, i.e. she has no idea at all.

Pierre told me that it wouldn't be easy to get acquainted

with her, unless I came up with something unusual. I thought and thought, but couldn't come up with anything except that I couldn't come up with anything. So now I am writing about how I cannot write, but I cannot write because I only write about how I cannot.

Pierre, my neighbour, is a writer. He is a man of medium height, handsome, with brown eyes and hair which is always tousled. Periodically, he advises me not to describe the appearance of characters, since the readers' imaginations have nothing else to do but imagine them themselves.

Pierre also said that if I couldn't think of anything unusual, then he would come up with something that would make Lucy decide to come to my place herself. At first I did not believe him, but he told me what to do: I just had to make different girls come to my apartment from time to time, and after a while, lower the curtain. The rest, he promised, was up to him.

Then he committed suicide, or perhaps was killed or simply died – you never can tell with writers. I am not that kind of a person, but I would like to be. I am still just writing about how I cannot write…

Besides, I don't very much believe that Lucy will come some day. Pierre is a writer, not a prophet, and things in life often don't happen like they do in the books…"

Lucy laughed. First she laughed at herself, next at Pierre, and then at Claude, who couldn't guess why she was laughing; he couldn't guess anything at all.

"Riddles again," said Lucy laughing. "Not bad at all…"

"Why are you laughing?" the words thrown into the air did not reach Claude because of the information vacuum he was in, "What's going on?"

(Here the Author reminds Lucy that one should say nothing but good of the dead.)

"Nothing" replied Lucy.

***

"I love sunsets," Pierre started talking with the first phrase he managed to recall from *Le Petit Prince*.

But the club meeting was already over, as well as the applause.

"Sunrise is no worse, I'd say. As for you, your face is very familiar to me," de Saint-Exupéry narrowed his eyes like someone who wants to recall something. "Have we met before?"

"No, definitely not in the previous life; maybe some time earlier," Pierre's joke was so lame that only Gwynplaine would be able to laugh (or whatever) at it.

Even that kind soul de Saint-Exupéry could only manage to smile.

"Maybe I'm wrong," de Saint-Exupéry shook his head and only after that he recalled that 'shaking one's head' was very stereotyped. "As they say, the only perfect rule is that nobody's perfect."

"It will be perfect," Pierre began and paused a little before playing *va banque*, "if you have to give something to me."

In response de Saint-Exupéry expressed the same emotion as Kazimir Malevich might have expressed on learning that his Black Square aroused worldwide admiration. In other words, he shrugged and asked in amazement: "Why?"

Now it was Pierre's turn to shrug.

"Wait a minute… I'll look through my notes – I'm putting down all the events of the day to remember them." De Saint-Exupéry took a notepad out of his pocket and opened it at the entries of the previous day.

"Here we are: *a stranger stopped me today and told me: 'Tomorrow, a man will approach you and ask you to give something to him', and he gave me a rolled paper which he took out of his pocket. I asked how I would recognise him, and he replied that the man himself would recognise me. Then he added: 'But, for goodness' sake, write down all this in a notepad so as not to forget.'* …Maybe you are the very man whom I should give something?"

Pierre knew for sure that the assumptions containing such phrases as 'maybe you are the very man' and 'give something' could never be very reliable, but he didn't know exactly what he was supposed to do, and decided to be 'the very man'.

(Here the Author thinks that long sentences are no better than a long tongue.)

"What did the stranger look like?" Pierre decided to get to the denouement at once, even without the Author's consent.

"Unfortunately, the only thing I remember is that I have memory problems," de Saint-Exupéry smiled and handed Pierre the rolled paper left by the stranger. "I easily forget everything. I may meet you in the street tomorrow and not recognise you… But wait a minute… can you tell me what is depicted in this picture?"

And he showed Pierre the same picture of the boa constrictor that had swallowed an elephant.

"A hat, of course!" said Pierre as he remembered that he should not remember the snake.

"Oh, how strange you, the grown-ups are..." murmured de Saint-Exupéry sadly. "It would be nice if we were born old and got younger by and by... Wouldn't it be wonderful if the light at the end of the tunnel was the light of the maternity ward where we are born?"

Going back to childhood reminded Pierre of Benjamin Button. Then he remembered that there was no use reminding de Saint-Exupéry about it, and in order to sooth him on leaving, told him only the following:

"Yeah, unfortunately, no grown-up will ever understand that this is a matter of so much importance!"

X

The Map of Literary Hell

Pierre had always appreciated maps attached to books. Firstly, because they always facilitate the perception of the narrative; secondly, they save from unnecessary descriptions (it is much better to consult the map than read: *In the southeast, two kilometres from Vanity Fair, there is the Colonel's Post which no one has been using for a long time)*; Thirdly, the maps are drawings, and the drawings are oases for tired eyes. Besides, along with all other advantages, maps always create an illusion of the situational complexity...

...One way or another, when Pierre unfolded the map handed over to him by de Saint-Exupéry and noticed (along with numbered items) a poem written on the reverse side, he guessed that the story was becoming more and more complicated:

Bestseller

233° CELSIUS
And like a duck now you avoid
Your own lagoon that has just frozen;
You're being spied on from the void,
But I can bet that you've chosen
Where to go, since you've guessed
What you're doing is for the best.

"Well, well… is there anything better to wish?" said Pierre and immediately remembered about a dozen other, more desirable things, "We have a map and encrypted places to be visited…"

"And we also have a hope that this is the last clue," sighed Conan Doyle like a depressed dinosaur[22] and took a closer look at the poem.

***

Pierre was always amazed at writers from olden times who wrote books seven hundred pages long and gave them titles like *David Copperfield* or *Anna Karenina*. True, in this way they immortalised their protagonists, but, to Pierre's mind, in the modern world, where so many books were written that a separate book could be dedicated to this phenomenon, the title was of great importance. *Harry Potter and the Secret Room* sounded more attractive than, for instance, *The Adventures of Harry Potter*; as well as the *The Hunger Games* seemed more exciting than *The Extraordinary Story of Peeta and Katniss*.

Certainly, the cover design and the name of the author were also of great importance, since Pierre knew one unshakable

---

22 You are not at all obliged to imagine how a depressed dinosaur sighs. (Sincere A/N)

truth of humanity: the main thing is to create a name, and then not only a book, but even a napkin with this name can be sold very easily. Though the title of the book, unconsciously (or maybe quite consciously), still played a greater role.

That was why Pierre always claimed that the title was like a business card...

***

"...if it's not outstanding in some way, nobody is going to pay any attention to it," said Pierre.

And truly, it was the title that led them to the Library of Dead Books; Anyway, they did not spend extra lines discussing that 233°C was 451.4°F.

The Library of Dead Books basically kept those works that were abandoned by readers halfway – the books that you start reading but, even with the thought "once I started, I'll read it to the end" can't read to the end. However, there were also the books whose vitality depended on the life span of the author's friends and relatives, and which were so boring that they could even compete with the sheep in the business of sending someone to sleep.

"I hope the clue is not left in any of these books," Conan Doyle wished in a voice befitting a lazy person, and in response to his wish (along with the old inscription – 'Looking for the top cruises? Call me. Ishmael') noticed a newly drawn letter **E**.

Bestseller

***

Choosing between a book and its screen version, Pierre was always for books. Probably because, as one great writer said, *first there was the word*, not a film frame. Nevertheless, Pierre suspected that in our century, in which people have no time to normally deal with not only books but also with their family, the films had one advantage over books – they took less time.

This was one of the reasons that the twenty-first century entailed book anorexia in the form of thin and short novels that could be started on the way to work and finished on the way back; that is, it took less time to read them than watch a film of a statistically average length.

Despite the fact that the era of thick books such as *Magic Mountain* was over, Pierre still continued to write thick books. As for reading, he preferred reading the thin ones.

***

The Catcher in the Rye was a thin book, and it was good too, so Pierre had read it several times. He loved this book but not so much as to kill Paul McCartney and then blame the book for it. Besides, the rebellious character Holden Caulfield seemed a bit comical in the new millennium and, to Pierre's mind, the main reason for admiring him was the inertia of elite opinion that the book should, by all means, be admired.

However, it proved to be useful. True, Pierre didn't know where the ducks flew when the lagoon in the Central Park of

New York froze,[23] but having read the first two lines of the poem (*And like a duck now you avoid your own lagoon that has just frozen*), he easily guessed where to go.

Casino 'Texas Holden', was situated on *Northanger Abbey Road* in Literary Hell. It enjoyed great popularity with the writers, since it was one of the greatest sources of literary ideas. The thing was that the gamblers needed to go there with ideas, not money: they could go inside with some meagre schemes for stories (e.g. 'A depressed cat decides to commit nine suicides but, eventually, he is so much carried away searching the various ways of committing them that he changes his mind' or 'In the world saturated with laziness due to new technologies, people are doing everything to do nothing') and, if the odds were not against them, could leave with great plots for novels. Though, as a rule, the majority of writers lost everything they had, thus making a great contribution to enriching the casino bank of ideas...

Pierre and Conan Doyle didn't go inside the building, since they could clearly see the letter **S** drawn on its wall.

***

Pierre rarely wrote about sex; he preferred experiencing it. Besides, he didn't want to sell his books only because they

---

23   Unanswered question which Holden Caulfield repeats throughout the whole novel. Unanswered question which Holden Caulfield repeats throughout the whole novel. Unanswered question which...

were written in '*spermanently* erotic language'. In other words, he preferred organic word combinations to descriptions of specific organs (firstly, as well as secondly and thirdly, because this niche was already comfortably occupied by Houellebecq).

He was also irritated with various religious manipulations of authors trying to symbolise Christ in their characters with banal hints about their age (thirty-three) or the number of their disciples (twelve). On the whole, such resemblances had no serious symbolic impact, but when readers read the passages from the gospels, they had an illusion of reading something 'profound', 'great', and 'divine'.

Little wonder with such an attitude Pierre could not gain popularity, thus running a risk of being forgotten and left without a monument...

***

...The monument of the Cuckoo's Nest (*You're being spied on from the void*) was one of the main sights in Literary Hell. It was an empty pedestal not only with no one to spy on you from it, but also with no nest as such. The same kind of a monument might be erected to Griffin or Tyler Durden. But even so, writers loved this monument – it is very 'symbolic,' they said, since they already knew the greatest axiom of the twenty-first century: *The main thing is not what you draw or sculpt, but the name you give to your creation*. Cuckoo's Nest monument justified its name perfectly. Moreover, if there really was a nest on the pedestal, it would seriously downplay the meaning embodied in it, and probably the adversary would not have chosen it as a landmark either.

This time, there flaunted the second newly-drawn letter **E** at the foot of the monument.

***

Pierre considered dialogues an integral part of the narrative. He would often compare novels with leisure parks and dialogues with the benches in them. "No matter how beautiful the park is," he used to say, "if you don't relax during a walk, you will quickly get tired."

As for the footnotes, he always fought against them. He often said that they were nothing more than the writer feeling superior to the reader, who, in the writer's opinion, had much less knowledge than he had.[24] He especially hated the books in which footnotes on some pages were longer than the text itself, and some of them even required a separate footnote. True, he understood those writers who put a deep and comprehensive meaning in their works and didn't want to lose it being unmarked in the footnotes, but, actually, he didn't really respect the deep and comprehensive meanings either.

However, he liked allusions. Certainly, those allusions should not be similar to say 'the rosebud rooted in the hair', that sounded like a literal translation of some unknown poem by some unknown romance poet, but neither should they be as trite or battered as the metaphorical calling for 'doing something without batting an eye'. He wanted something between

---

24 *Life like that in a Film,* 2010, Pierre Sonnage: p.121, line 5.

radical intellectualism and primitive patterns. But Pierre did not realise that he'd better give up poking his nose in other people's footnotes or allusions, and deal with the meanings embedded in his own books, speaking metaphorically, of course.

***

I can bet that you've chosen was too primitive; more primitive than the Amoeba cell structure or the difference between Coca-Cola and Pepsi-Cola.[25]

The Shakespearean Betting House *Mac-Bet* was the best place to make a profit in the whole of Literary Hell. The writers here made bets on everything: which profession would the murderer in the new detective novel by Agatha Christie belong to, who would become a Nobel Prize winner in the big bright world, which writers would die earlier than others and move very soon to Literary Hell, and so on.

Be it some other time, Pierre would also bet with pleasure, but now he had no time to spare on biblioptic forecasts, especially since this once the author of the messages showed great lexical generosity, and to prove his existence, wrote *three* letters – CHE – on the wall of *Mac-Bet*.

25 Here the Author alluded to Coehlo's *Eleven Minutes* – the book in which a character (before speaking about high matters), admits that he can only distinguish Coca-Cola from Pepsi-Cola. This allusion is made only because the Author believes that Coehlo would never have imagined that his words would be alluded to by someone else. But the Author has a very kind heart.

Apparently, even Hell kept pace with what was in fashion on Earth.

***

Pierre could never explain why something was becoming popular. He did not understand how the Black Square differed from the Red Circle painted by his neighbour Jean, or what made the line drawn by Picasso better than the beam drawn by Jean. Moreover, he couldn't explain why something became popular just because its author died one day.

By and by he realised that the earth rotated round PR, and that everything could be sold including me, you, him, her, it, us, and them. Consequently, if someone could not sell his products, he had to sell himself. Pierre always lacked PR and hoped in vain that in a world drowning in an ocean of printed matter that his books would emerge on the surface the moment they were published. Therefore, no one gave him the Nobel Prize or the hope that he would ever get it.

Eventually Pierre realised that there was no sacrifice too big to get good publicity, even the ultimate sacrifice of committing suicide. And he committed it.

***

"So, what have we got now?" Conan Doyle inquired in such a tone that it didn't even require a question mark.

"CHE-E-S-E," answered Pierre and took an imaginary photo with an imaginary camera.

"i.e.?"[26]

"i.e., our Graffiti artist turned out to be an ordinary graphomaniac," replied Pierre being in the same mood as Louis XVI of France who stood by the guillotine and remembered that he himself had introduced this device. "He did it for zilch, maybe just to make fun of us."

"Nothing is done for zilch," Conan Doyle uttered such unsuccessful wisdom that the Author was even ashamed. "The dog's bone is buried somewhere else. No one would have sent us to four different places in vain."

Pierre had no choice but to agree that he had no other choice. So he went back to the map.

"Maybe we should combine these four points to see something important?"

Conan Doyle liked the idea, but he soon had to reject it, since connecting the points they got an image of such a strange pipe that even René Magritte[27] would envy them.

(Here the Author sighed and decided to brighten Pierre's mind for the last time.)

Right at that moment, quite unexpectedly, Pierre guessed that he had guessed something…

***

A bestseller is not a particularly good book, but it's neither

---

26 If only he could ever get rid of that terrible 'i.e!' (worried A/N)

27 Actually, this is not a footnote; the Author simply wants to say that he means the painting by René Magritte, which depicts a pipe with the inscription under its image: *'Ceci n'est pas une pipe'* (This is not a pipe).

bad, of course. It's something like the fact that happiness is not in money, but it is not entirely in the lack of money either.

Pierre often wondered what turned the book into a bestseller and what was the reason that people read any of King's books more often than *Ulysses*. He also believed that King could never compete with Joyce, but the fact remained the fact while his meditations merely his meditations.

Gradually he realised that in the modern world no one had enough nerves to unravel Joyce's multi-layered ideas; he realised that people's life was already burdened so much that it could not be burdened further; and in the end he also realised that for a bestseller it was not necessary to perpetuate deep philosophical thoughts in the texts – all that was needed proved to be a good title, original cover, popular author, small amount of text, narration without any allusions, minimal footnotes and PR.

(Here the Author wants to ask Pierre whether he has been thinking long to come up with this brilliant conclusion... but this time he decides to leave the poor soul alone.)

However, the only bad moment in all this lyrical and wise conclusion was that Pierre started everything from the end, right from PR, so he had too little time and space for writing a bestseller (not to speak of publishing it) – about a hundred and fifty floors' distance and time respectively, needed for descending from the roof of the skyscraper to its foot...

***

"Look," Pierre pointed to the map, "all places have names, and only some of them have numbers. This means that…"

"What's important is not where you go, but what numbers are those places marked with!" Conan Doyle was tired of playing Watson's part.

But Pierre never liked numbers or maths. He was sure that neither Cotangent alpha nor the logarithmic equations would ever be useful to him in life, let alone the calculation of the perimeters and areas of objects of strange shapes. He believed that mathematics would never become a vital science and, therefore, to study by heart the formulae was less important than learning the techniques of, say, mouth-to-mouth breathing, which might be of some use.

Despite such scepticism, it was the case where the clue was hidden in the very numbers.

"Right you are, here the numbers are important. 1.9.8.4. At times I think that our adversary hasn't read anything but Orwell's books."

"This is where the map will come into play," Conan Doyle decided to view the events positively and poked his finger at the spot with the inscription 'BBC' – Big Brother's Channel.

The storyline was definitely approaching the climax.

XI

Po(e)stmodernism

"Life is like Forrest Gump – it moves pretty fast."

Memento Moriarty, 2008, Pierre Sonnage

'Big Brother's Channel' was the only broadcaster in Literary Hell. It was located in a small building but did great things – its surveillance cameras, installed in every corner of the area, forced the writers to take part in one big reality show. The show was based on a simple principle: anyone could choose anyone they wanted to watch, and their TV, at certain times of the day, automatically showed fragments of the chosen writer's life. In other words, this was the only television in the entire universe that could watch the viewers themselves and, at certain periods of time, give them the opportunity to watch other viewers as well.

The television was run by Big Brother who managed to direct it so that no one, including George Orwell, had ever seen him. Moreover, no one had any idea who he was. Some even thought that Big Brother did not exist at all, and that he was invented by George Orwell to rule the people more easily; while others believed that on the contrary – he was everywhere and would show up only when he was not expected.

Such were Big Brother and his television channel, which transmitted only two types of programmes: yellow and informational. The function of the informational programme was to show what life was like in Literary Hell, while the yellow programme turned this life into hell.

When Pierre and Conan Doyle entered the television building, the news programme was being transmitted: "Chronicle of a Death Foretold! Tonight the famous Colombian writer Gabrielle Garcia Marquez arrives in hell," the presenter said with a satisfied face. "The autumnal patriarch is already awaited at the gates by friends, melancholy whores and fans. We will soon switch to the gates, but until then…"

"You again?" said George Orwell instead of 'hello' when he came out into the foyer, "What are you looking for this time?"

(At this point not only Conan Doyle and Pierre but also the Author were at a loss, since the only fragile thread of hope they had [apart from acid, of course]

indicated that Orwell should have known at least something.)

"Aren't there any messages or letters left for us?" Pierre resorted to a method tested on de Saint-Exupéry.

There were not.

"Today. Edgar Alan Poe's. Annual festival. *Po(e)stmodernism is held.* The modern minimalist works. Will be presented..." Ernest Hemingway spoke in short sentences specific to his style. "I would single out. Minimalist story by O. Henry. *Silence.* Ending where it starts..."

"Would you let us view the recordings on the cameras?" Pierre tried for the second time to come to the denouement in a roundabout way.

He wouldn't.

"...and here's another minimalist story. *Shepherd.* Shepherd did not have to take a nap. He lost two sheep per night. He was entrusted forty-four sheep, but he did not even remember how many were left. One. Two. Three. Four... He fell asleep at twenty-five..." Hemingway continued to read minimalist stories. "Here is presented poetry too. Though personally, I prefer prose. Over the *Dead Poets Society*..."

There came the moment when Pierre and Conan Doyle felt that they had to shake a leg, but someone was still pulling their legs.

"Look!" Pierre screamed all of a sudden pointing to the graffiti behind Hemingway on the screen. It was a fresh drawing; moreover – it was unfinished, still in progress... and a hooded person was working on it with great care.

(How did I notice that the stranger was doing it with 'great care', I wonder? – A/N)

"It's him!" Pierre exclaimed with such relief, as Newton would while running a hand over his aching head and assuring himself that he had no lump. "We need to hurry! Let's put our best foot forward!"

"So, Come to the Festival. You're all welcome to Black Square..." Hemingway addressed the camera, while the man behind him was so carried away with drawing, that he didn't pay attention to what was going on around him. "See you soon..."

Black Square was quite close to the television building. So it didn't take Pierre and Conan Doyle long (despite the shortness of breath) to get there running. Although the artist had already managed to finish his job – the familiar name 'Poe' was already written in an unfamiliar font on the wall.

"I think it's time to find out who is behind all this," Pierre said and headed for the hooded stranger.

***

*"Love is a strange thing – you hope
your faith in it will move mountains,
but when the time comes, you're unable to say even
three little words: I love you."*

Pierre Sonnage, 2006, *Homo Faberge*

Claude and Lucy met at Café *Jean-Paul Sartre*. It could not be said that this place was especially attractive to him or her, but for Lucy the main thing was that the name included the letter combination 'art', and for Claude the very fact of meeting Lucy. Therefore, none of them felt uneasy there.

Claude knew that, unlike written speech, in oral speech you shouldn't talk about the fact that you can't talk. Therefore, he kept silent. Lucy knew that every story, even the most extraordinary, required at least one love affair, but she had nothing to say and was silent too.

To put it otherwise, the force of gravity on the earth turned out to be stronger than silence, so the silence fell quite heavily.

Claude also knew that often, when a person wants to say a lot, he cannot say even a little, because in such cases each sentence is like a move in chess – one wrong decision and the advantage will immediately pass to the opponent.

Although, at that moment Claude didn't really think about chess. He just felt love and thought that if he opened his mouth to say something, a butterfly would fly out there.

In general, Claude thought less and felt more. He felt that there was no time for thinking and thought that he had to express his feelings verbally. It was precisely for this reason that he forgot the whole text that he had thought up in advance, took a very deep breath, not taking into account the dimensions of his lungs, and said:

"…"

"No," Lucy interrupted him until he uttered a word, "it's better to put full stop to all this matter at the beginning."

"I have put full stop to our relationship so many times that in the end I got an ellipsis, so I continued," Claude answered, and thought that he should remember this phrase to include it in some story.

"Look here," continued Lucy, "I have a different opinion about love. I love alternative rock, since it has no alternative; I love modernism in literature, since it isn't modern any longer; I like photography, since I look great in all my selfies; I love Elite culture, because I don't know why I love it; I love T-shirts with the image of *Star Wars* characters, because it is fashionable to love them without even watching a single episode... Generally, I love a lot, and all my feelings have a special reason. But I can't fall in love with you just for the reason that it is favourable for the plot..."

"Then why was it necessary to introduce me to the plot at all?" Claude was confused. "Nothing happens in books for no reason. Even the episodic appearance of a character described in a single line has some connection with the whole story."

"I don't know," Lucy shrugged, "Probably because not everything should necessarily have a happy end..."

"But I love you!"

(Bravo, bravo! – A/N)

"I, too... want to love you, but love is not wheat to sow and harvest in autumn," said Lucy and immediately realised that it sounded very stupid.

"Lucy, we already have a story that deserves a happy ending..."

"Or becoming part of history!"

"So, you are as impenetrable as the Thermopylae passage," said Claude and guessed that making an original comparison in such a situation was as stupid as choosing 'Thermopylae passage' for that purpose. "It's a pity, because we could turn a lot of pleasant experiences into pleasant memories, because life is the sum of emotions and not days. When you deny pleasant moments because of fear of the future, you miss the short minutes that are better than a whole week lived without any emotions at all…"

"How shiny the surface of this spoon is," said Lucy, admiring her image in the spoon and straightening her hair. "Let's take a selfie in it."

***

"I think it's time to find out who is behind all this," Pierre tried to create the same effect that is often found in TV series, when after the intrusion of ads, they repeat the phrase from the previous episode.

"For the time being, it's us who are behind him," Conan Doyle uttered thinking that he had come up with a very witty answer, and stepped aside to let Pierre approach the hooded stranger.

It suddenly occurred to Pierre that to finish the story simply with going up to the stranger, putting a hand on his shoulder, turning him round, and removing the hood from his head would be very commonplace; that their long searches would lose all meaning; that it was just an oversight from the criminal, and that it was not at all fitting for Sir Arthur Ignatius Conan Doyle to come to such a primit…

And a suspicion that had been orbiting him like Phobos and Deimos all the time struck him surprisingly hard: Sir

Arthur Ignatius Conan Doyle… SAICD…

ACIDS!

"Ah, there it is! How couldn't I have guessed it so far!" thought Pierre and turned to Conan Doyle:

"You…"

And suddenly something struck him again, this time due to a strong blow given by his companion with whom he had been going hand in hand throughout all those hardships… The blow was very strong.

"Finita la commedia," whispered Pierre and fell on the ground without making a noise…

POET

…Noticing nothing, the hooded stranger went on drawing peacefully. He drew black T to red POE – the official name of the poetic part of the Poe's festival.

***

Claude thought that love was a mere attachment, and that people often lacked patience to get to the point of that attachment. He lacked it too. He wanted to find out everything then and there, right in the café.

"So, do you mean is it over forever?" he tried to bring artificial drama into the conversation, since the word 'forever', to some extent, always affects the human subconscious.

"True, we should never say never, but…" the dialogue has

long demanded this phrase and Lucy said it. "I think nothing will come of it, we shall never be together."

"How do you, girls, always know in advance what will happen in the future?" Claude decided to solve the problem of the centuries-old secret embedded in the female genetic code within a minute.

"I know, because I like a different kind of boys..."

"How different?"

Lucy was confused. As a rule, with others this was a winning argument and no one tried to clarify further.

"Just different."

"And what kind of a boy am I?"

Lucy was even more confused, because she neither knew what kind of a boy Claude was, nor what he had to be to fall in love with him.

"Enough!" Lucy took advantage of the unique rule of rejecting unanswerable questions. "We tried to introduce a line of love into this complicated story, but it didn't work. So we need to put an end to it."

"Okay..." Claude's face expressed the same as Hitler's face would have expressed when he failed the exam at the Academy of Fine Arts. "But we can't put an end to it, since I live on the opposite side of your street. You're in habit of watching, and you won't be able to give up this habit immediately and forever. You'll get used to me. First you'll just know that I love you and will live in peace. But then you will find out that I have another girlfriend. You will see it from the window and get angry first with me, and then yourself, because you'll understand that you have no reason to be mad at me. Then you'll come to me again, just like yesterday. So, I don't quite understand what's the point of suffering so much if the result is going to be the same."

"I'm leaving tomorrow," said Lucy, who did not know whether to smile or not. "I'm moving to Paris."

XII

Playing with Fire

Pierre came to his senses in a very unusual situation; unusual in the sense that he found himself in a small, almost empty room, with a noose round his neck.

Conan Doyle was the first to come to his mind, but the context in which he remembered him was by no means pleasant. He could not believe that his once beloved author had been deceiving him, that he was standing in front of the one who stood behind all this, and standing behind all that was before it... After a while, Pierre stopped thinking about the exact position of Conan Doyle, as it was going to grow into a pornographic passage, and started thinking about the identity of his main adversary.

Next he realised that there was a noose around his neck. "I started with suicide and they make me end with suicide," he smiled, since no man ever stepped in the same Hell twice.[28]

Then he noticed a looking glass on the opposite wall and a TV above it. A hatched circle was drawn on the looking glass. "One more riddle, and I'll go crazy," Pierre thought and instantly guessed that something worse than that was threatening him.

The TV turned on.

There appeared Poe on the screen. He looked exactly as in the old pictures – chronically sad, with a heart-piercing look in his eyes. However, he had spiralled circles on the cheeks drawn with a red lipstick.

(Oh Gosh! Hollywood has completely driven people crazy! A/N)

"Well, now everything has become clear! Although I already knew it for sure!" Pierre thought, and immediately realised that he did not know it for sure at all; maybe only suspected, since

---

28 'No man ever steps in the same river twice,' Heraclitus announced once, and the Author remembered it in order to use it in a different context some day.

Poe was nowhere to be seen, but his presence was everywhere – in the hotel (NEVERMORE), in his own house, and at the festival he organised himself. He also planned the party and appeared to the guests wearing a hoodie not to be recognised. Besides, so that his absence at the party wouldn't seem strange, he pretended to be missing... and Conan Doyle must have knocked out Pierre before he recognised the villain... Damn it!

"Hello, Pierre," said Edgar Allan Poe, who hadn't uttered a single word till then. "First of all, I want to congratulate you on the fact that you proved to be cleverer than I thought, but not as clever as you thought. Throughout this time the rising action was leading to the climax, and here you are, with a noose around your neck, left high and dry."

"I want to play a game..."

"People always think that they have a long life to live, but they never have enough time to live the life they want. Actually, time is too short – what is future at the present moment, turns into past a moment later..."

"It seems here, too, everyone is a philosopher," thought Pierre, and if there was not the noose around his neck, he would even shake his head in disapproval.

"Have you ever thought about what you could do in a minute?"

Pierre hadn't.

"...You could go down from the fiftieth floor, if you exit through the window instead of the door..."

"...Run the distance that Usain Bolt runs in ten seconds, or even count to thirty twice..." Pierre tried to help Poe.

"Well," Poe smiled so faintly that even the Author hardly

noticed it. "I wonder if you will be in the same good mood in a minute, since you have only sixty seconds to name the person who started much ado about nothing. Only in that case you'll get the strength to get rid of that noose; or else you'll burn at the stake."

(Here the Author realises that watching Hollywood films proves to be pretty dangerous for him as well.)

Poe disappeared from the monitor, and a stopwatch appeared there.

Fifty-nine…

Fifty-eight…

And Pierre guessed that all those books and films in which characters manage to concentrate in a critical situation and make the right decision with a cool mind merely lied. The only thing he could think about was that in a minute, waiting for a flame of fire to appear from all four corners of the room, it was impossible to come up with the right answer which he had been looking for in vain for so long.

Fifty…

Forty-nine…

Pierre tried hard to recall everything that had happened since he arrived in Literary Hell. But it was his entire life that flashed before his eyes, and he could not concentrate on two fronts at the same time.

"Conan Doyle!" he uttered the first name that occurred to him, but the noose was getting tighter.

Forty…

Thirty-nine…

"Poe!" he exclaimed. But that did not help either, although he thought it certainly would.

Thinking about the name, for some reason he thought about what he would say to humanity if only a few minutes were left before the end of the world, but then he realised that this was romantic nonsense, and it was better to think about his own demise.

Thirty-two…

Thirty-one…

"Antoine de Saint-Exupéry… Hemingway… Orwell… Hugo… Dante… Bradbury…" he named everyone he remembered, but alas…

There was left neither time nor space.

Twenty-eight…

Twenty-seven…

For the first time, he felt sorry that Bruce Willis did not choose a writer's career and did not die.

Twenty-four…

Twenty-three…

The fire was approaching him. Pierre felt that he was as helpless as Samson might have been on leaving the barber's, and did what people generally do for self-rescue – fainted…

***

Lucy was disappointed. All began so excitingly, but ended with only a young man falling in unrequited love.

These boys always spoil everything! she wrote. *It seems everything is going well… but no! One day they fall in love without even asking permission!*

In fact, Lucy was simply afraid of love. Firstly, because she had never experienced true love, and secondly, because the love shown in books and films rarely coincided with what could be seen in real life (like an attractively advertised hamburger, which in reality may turn out to be tasteless or past its sell-by date).

Apart from this, she was also afraid of being left without love. Firstly, because love, or rather its absence, was already what she felt, and secondly, because in films and books people without love showed the real state of things much better than… well, the yummy hamburger they promised.

Therefore, Lucy always ran away to avoid things – first, she tried to avoid talking with others, then she tried to avoid those others themselves. But she never succeeded, as if in a nightmare, when you run, run, but cannot run away. Even if you run away from someone, then someone else will surely appear, and you will have to run away again. In short, Lucy was afraid of love, to be left without love, and even of the fact that she could never overcome herself and get rid of at least one of these fears.

…Being a persistent runaway, she was used to packing things very quickly. So she packed the necessary things in no time, and fled.

***

Pierre came to himself in a few seconds, but found out that nothing had changed: he was still standing with a noose around his neck, and burning in the same fire.

Bestseller

(Small wonder he was! A/N)

The only way out seemed to be in the looking-glass, or rather in the hatched circle drawn on it...

...Pierre never liked numbers or maths. He believed that mathematics would never become a vital science...

...but now he realised that he was wrong. Therefore, he also realised that he had two news – good and bad: The good news was that he remembered the hatched part meant something, and the bad news was that he remembered nothing more.

Twelve...

Eleven...

"Mathematics kills!" Pierre dumped his ignorance on the exact science, and did the most stupid thing that could have been done in that situation – he began to scrutinise himself in the mirror. He never once looked at himself since he arrived in hell, after all... It turned out that he hadn't changed much. Only a new scar had appeared on his face (he ran his hand along the hollow on his forehead), probably left after that terrible blow. The scar was narrow and looked like the strait between Scylla and Charybdis...

"Aha!" This time Pierre understood everything without the Author's intervention. Accordingly, the main episodes flashed before his eyes one after another in dim pictures, as it happens in films...

...A stranger running out of the room, whose face seemed familiar to him though he could only caught a glimpse of it...

De Saint-Exupéry with a bewildered gaze and his perplexed hypothesis – "Your face is familiar to me. Have we met before?"

...Hugo's significant phrase: "Like a narrow strait between Scylla and Charybdis..."

...Besides, they would not hang a mirror and draw a hatched circle for no reason...

...Conan Doyle must also have struck him to prevent him from seeing the face of the man in a hoodie, as he would have understood that it wasn't Poe, but...

Five...

Four...

And Pierre, who already claimed to be the heir to Jeanne Dark and Giordano Bruno, suddenly exclaimed:

"Pierre Sonnage!"

And the noose round his neck loosened.

XIII

$$S = \pi r^2$$

Poe hated the sentences beginning with the phrase 'I have to ask you for a favour' as much as happy days, and his heart would sink three times at least before the author of the phrase passed from it to the favour itself. Firstly, he really did not like 'to help,' as an infinitive, and even more so as an action; secondly, requests beginning in this form were prerequisite for pretty difficult tasks.

So, when Mephistopheles visited him one ugly day and began his speech directly with, 'I have to ask you for a favour,' Poe's heart sank deep into his stomach – refusing Mephistopheles was more difficult than accepting his offer.

"The newcomer's name is Pierre. He committed suicide quite recently – jumped from the tallest building in the world. He has only a few small scars, which he got due to malfunction of LHD.[29] His heart stopped a few minutes before landing, so he was already dead when he hit the asphalt. We must prepare his punishment before he wakes up. For that we have to divide him into two, as we'll need two Pierres."

"Why me?" Poe couldn't imagine that someone still remembered his William Wilson.[30]

"Because Palahniuk is still alive,"[31] Mephistopheles answered briefly. "Hurry up! It's *His* personal order…"

It was not difficult to create Pierre's *doppelgänger*, since Pierre was lying on the table obedient like Dolly the sheep.

"Hurry up!" Poe started giving orders in his turn. "Both will come to their senses in no time. Take the first one to the gates, let him think that he fell right there. Dante will take care of him from the first, and then pass him to Conan Doyle. I will take the other Pierre to the hotel and keep an eye on him myself. Remember that they mustn't see each other until we get to the end, otherwise everything will go to hell. Warn Conan Doyle to act like a fool; it's easier for fools to gain trust, you know… Well, come on now, we don't have much time!"

…Opening his eyes Pierre thought he would see a traditional picture of the hospital lights flickering on the ceiling, but alas! Despite the fact that he had fallen from the

---

29 LHD – Literary Hell Delivery – is the company providing the delivery of souls from earth to hell.

30 No wonder he couldn't, because the Author himself had to consult google to recall Poe's character fighting with his *doppelgänger*.

31 God grant him a long life if he writes such books as *Fight Club* (the Author's indir. Note)

147th floor, he was lying in bed in one piece, and the person standing in front of him did not resemble a doctor.

Although, not only that but…

"Welcome your soul to Literary Hell! I am Edgar Allan Poe, and my name must be familiar to you, methinks. Let me go straight to the point," Poe went straight to the point, as there was too little time left. "So, this is Literary Hell, as I've told you. *Why, How,* and *What for* should be asked later. Here the writers are tortured exactly in the same way as they used to torture their readers while being alive…"

Pierre tried to recall his twelve readers.

"Riddles… puzzles… sometimes they are okay, and often fit well in the narrative, but even if one has a sweet tooth he's bored with eating cakes all the time, you know."

Coming up with pseudo-philosophical maxims was one of Edgar Poe's hobbies.

"These sophisticated stories of yours are also boring, believe me, but until you experience all this in person, you won't understand it…"

Pierre shivered as if he had heard the unpleasant sound of a fork scratching a plate.

"In short, your punishment will be like this: you have to make a puzzle that can turn a person's life into hell," said Poe, and paused, as he liked to look into people's frightened eyes…

"Whose?" Pierre wondered, not missing the chance to insert an interrogative pronoun into the conversation.

"It's still a secret," Poe answered with such an air that would guarantee him the role of James Bond in a film by any rational film director. "He will be here very soon, but mind, if he sees you, if he turns out to be cleverer than you are, you will have to endure such a horrible punishment that this Hell will seem paradise to you!"

(As if Conan Doyle's permanent "That's it"-s and "i.e."-s were not enough, now there appeared Poe's repeated "hell"-s!)

"Therefore, stay away from him and try to work out the code whose answer will lead him to me..." Poe went on hastily. "Conan Doyle also wrote a kind of a cipher on the mirror, but don't pay attention to it; you should only mind your own business... I'll tell you the rest when you come to my place. I live in Rue Morgue. Here's the map which will help you find my house easily. Is everything clear?"

It was not entirely clear, but even so Pierre nodded in agreement, as he had no other way out.

"Play Hell with him," said Poe and left the room with a sly smile. Pierre immediately picked up a sheet of paper, strained his mind as if recalling something, and began to write:

"DECANON
1) Do not write thick books..."

***

Claude never understood why people committed suicide because of love. Accordingly, he was amused by Anna Karenina, who fought for almost a thousand pages just to jump under the wheels of a train in the end. However, when the window on the seventh floor of the house on the opposite side remained dark, he decided to see a completely different light at the end of the tunnel.

So what, that he was only twenty-five; so what, that he had already chosen his way; so what, that there were other girls; so what, that he had his own apartment; so what, that he dreamed of becoming a writer and even felt that he had some chance of it if he stopped writing only about how he could not write; so what, that… Claude stopped thinking, or else a couple of more 'so what-s,' and he would change his mind about committing suicide, thus ending everything very banally.

He did not think about the method of committing it for a long time, since the formula 'if you cannot commit suicide, kill yourself because you cannot commit it' would not work here. "Nothing is universal in the world," Claude thought, "including the phrase that nothing is universal in the world."

He opened the window. One step forward and… "No," Claude retorted to himself, "first I need to shout 'Geronimo' and jump only after that." And pleased that he had clarified what to do, he stepped onto the windowsill.

"If only I were an important character in this story, the phone would ring now!" Claude said for the Author's ears, most likely. But he forgot that he didn't have a phone at home and, in addition, he left his mobile phone in a taxi that morning… "I always thought that any character, even a bit-part one described in a single line, was of some importance…"

(And while the Author thinks where to get the phone from and how to make it ring just at this very moment, before Claude jumps out of the window…)

…Claude moved forward a little…

(And when the Author tried to calm himself down thinking Claude knew that it was not worthwhile to commit suicide because of Lucy…)

…Suddenly a light came on in Lucy's window and someone shouted: "Stop!"

***

Pierre never really loved Lucy. Maybe because he thought love was the ideal way of wasting time. But he liked flirting, as well as having one (or maximum two) night stand, not requiring walking hand in hand, constant corresponding, and calling each other 'darling' or 'babe'.

He did not love Lucy, but he liked it when people loved each other, and that was why he started this game with her. The inclusion of an encrypted message in the book included a certain risk of not decrypting, but it was impossible to interest Lucy otherwise, which meant that Claude would have remained alone in his apartment with his excessive shyness…

…But that was before. Now Pierre faced a more serious challenge: his adversary was unfamiliar to him, which made him more dangerous, since the mystery often indicates strength rather than weakness. Therefore, Pierre decided to deliver precision strikes on the enemy and dash and dot his hopes.

…Just the moment when he put the last dot, he heard the sound of footsteps in the corridor…

"I must hurry up," he thought. Someone was already

standing in the doorway. Pierre did not even have time to carefully examine his face, as he had to rush out of the room. Running away he felt that someone was running after him. Then the lights went off, and till his chaser managed to shed light on everything, Pierre was already on the safe side.

***

"Books that you read and films that you watch, don't exist. You exist only in what you do."

Federico Fellini, or maybe not.

It wasn't Lucy.

Why should it be? If Claude really wanted Lucy back, he would have rushed after her to the station, changing many means of transport on his way, breaking many laws including traffic rules, pushing through crowds of people at the station and, having still missed the train, would have sadly returned to the waiting room to see Lucy there biting her lower lip and smiling shyly.

And he would have definitely seen her, because Lucy was a filmosopher and believed that any film contained some meaning (even a stupid one, such as realised in the previous paragraph) and, therefore, she missed the Cannes-Paris train. Seeing Claude, they would have kissed and lived happily if not ever after, then at least for a few years.

But when Claude not only did not appear at the station, but almost followed the train to see a different light at the end of the tunnel, she realised that she was an idiot – she should at least have learned his last name and written down his contact information; she shouldn't have given up her apartment for rent so easily telling everything about Claude to a new tenant who had all the qualities to make him fall in love with her...

...Audrey, in fine fettle, was already standing in front of Claude in his apartment, trying to convince him of the banal truth that suicide was not an option.

"I understand you, Claude. Lucy told me everything," her voice sounded somewhat optimistic. "I know that you have depression, and that you have already tried four times to commit suicide..."

"What?" Claude was so surprised by the last sentence that he even forgot about the non-existent depression.

"Yes, sweetheart. And she also told me that you have memory problems but try to deny it," she went on. "Everything that happens is always logical, believe me. I know how you feel. A little earlier, I was also going to end my life, with the same method as you..."

...Claude raised his head and looked at Audrey for the first time.

"Yes, yes... When I was going up in the lift, a man entered as well. He bent over to me and said that everyone had their own Calvary. I realised at once that it was a sign from above and that there were no unsolved problems in life. The man was so full of optimism and sounded so convincing, that I changed my mind and left the lift on my floor. So, I lost neither my life, nor the pleasure of being in Dubai."

"In Dubai, you say?" Claude asked the most inappropriate question that could be asked after hearing Audrey's story.

"Exactly. For some reason I wanted to jump from the

tallest building in the world," she laughed. "There mustn't be any other idiot who might think about this before committing suicide."

Claude smiled. Now he was convinced that there was at least one character mentioned in a single line at the beginning of the story, who turned out to be very important. He even noticed that Audrey was a pretty girl.

"By the way, I'm doing nothing special tomorrow evening," she added. Claude, too, was not very busy... by the way.

"Now, logically, we should kiss," thought Claude and leaned toward Audrey, but...

...Suddenly the phone rang...

"Where did this phone come from? I never had one," Claude wondered...

(Here the Author got terribly upset, as he forgot to change his mind about the phone. Therefore, embarrassed by his irresponsibility, he hastily left the room and even closed the curtains... just in case.)

***

It has never been difficult for Pierre to speak publicly. Although, when he appeared before writers whom until then he knew only by the name written on the book covers, he realised that it would be really hard to meet their great expectations...

..."Hell yeah, the black box is a very good idea!" Poe praised Pierre on returning to the dining room. "Now you urgently need to find de Saint-Exupéry."

"Dear me! I would gladly sell my soul to the devil only to have a chance of meeting him!"

"Be careful! Speak of the devil, and he is bound to appear!" Poe smiled recalling the business of the second-hand souls.

***

(Here the Author suddenly began thinking about the idea of his book. He thought, and thought, and thought, and in the end he thought that it didn't seem worth thinking much about it. So he went on writing.)

***

Pierre had never dealt with drawing or painting; maybe only in his childhood when his future was painted in bright colours (and even then only figuratively, of course). So he was amazed when he managed to draw the colour letters on the walls so masterfully…

He was just finishing his last piece of graffiti when he heard a faint sound and a loud sigh of someone standing behind him. He didn't look back, but not because he was afraid to turn into a pillar of salt, merely because it was clear that the plan was being fulfilled successfully – his adversary had to drop out of the game just when he had only to take the last step to finish. Consequently, he carried out his duty perfectly, and now it was Edgar Allan Poe's turn to appear.

"We are close to the end," admitted Poe who had just turned up.

"At last!" Pierre was eager to learn who was the poor soul with whom he raised Hell and thus escaped a hard punishment himself.

"Now you'll meet your adversary very soon, if he was able to cope with his problem, of course," said Poe, and smiled like an evil Cartoon character who swallowed the door key of the room in which he had locked his victim. "But at first we should light a fire – it's a cold day in hell."

XIV

Bestseller

"They say God is great and omnipotent. They also say that in the beginning he created the heavens and the earth, and on the sixth day he created man. Yes, the same man who, later and in stages, invented paper, writing script, weapons, printing, the conveyer belt, cars, computers, televisions, telescopes... and even God himself, since he was not able to see him in the sky with his telescope."

Memento Moriarty, 2008, Pierre Sonnage

Pierre had never dreamed of having a twin. Moreover, he was sometimes even annoyed to see his own reflection in the looking-glass. Therefore, when the noose fell off his neck, the fire went out and the game was over, he was taken aback to see the second Pierre when leaving the room.

Pierre had never dreamed of having a twin. Moreover, he was sometimes even annoyed to see his own reflection in the looking-glass. Nevertheless, when he saw himself coming out of the room, he was so confused that he could not even figure out how confused he should be...

"I couldn't imagine that anything else would surprise me here," said one of Pierres with an expression of someone to whom the basics of quantum physics were explained.

"I hope, somebody will explain to us what's going on here," said the other one, whom we thought to be the first Pierre.

That somebody turned out to be Poe, who entered the room as if on call.

"Creating a *doppelgänger* was Jules Verne's innovative project," he began in 'you-two-should-have-guessed-about-this-long-ago' tone. "The arithmetic paradox – one equals two... while for you it's just a punishment. As I told you... or maybe I told it to one of you?... Anyway, as I've already said, you tormented the reader with endless riddles, so it was not difficult to come up with a proper punishment for you and put both of you through Hell – one Pierre had to make a riddle and the other had to solve it, and both of you suffered because one is the other, or vice versa... Now you can sit together like the Brothers Grimm and write anything you wish till *He* comes up with a new punishment for you."

"*He?*" asked both Pierres simultaneously.

"Exactly. *He* always plans punishments," Poe answered

yawning and stretching like his cat, "while my punishment is to carry out his plans under Mephistopheles' supervision."

"The plans of Big Brother?" the first Pierre was insistent.

"No, Big Brother never shows up, he only watches us," Poe said and bit his tongue in a desperate effort to say nothing more.

"And what is going to be the next punishment?" inquired the other Pierre who was as curious as the first one.

"Can't fink of anyfing," Poe answered happy for finding the method of tongue-biting.

Pierres shrugged. Now they were calmer, perhaps because two heads are better than one.

"So you can live anywhere in Hell and do anything you like for a while," said Poe loosening his tongue, "I still have a lot to do. I have to make 99 clones of Anna Frank before Beigbeder arrives and takes care of them…"

Pierres had no idea what to say, so they said the phrase pretty illogical for Hell and too banal for the end: "Thank god it all ended well!"

"How lovely you are," Poe's eyes lit up, "You remind me of one of my old dreams about how good it would be if a person had two hearts like many other organs."

"So that he could love more, right?" asked the second Pierre whose only heart softened.

"No, to double the chance of a myocardial infarction," Poe answered, and left as hastily as he had come.

***

"Pierre Sonnage told me that when I am not able to write anything, I should write about how I can't write, then remove the first paragraph, and everything will be all right. So I'll try it.

However, I don't have much to write about at present. I simply wanted to say that the secondary character as such does not exist, since it is impossible to call someone 'secondary' if someone else becomes the protagonist thanks to him.

What's going on with me now seems very unusual. I have seen such things only in the films. Who knows, maybe life can sometimes be like a film…"

***

"No, life is definitely not a film," Lucy wrote. *"I thought I was the main character, but in the end it turned out that my only function was to leave my apartment to someone else… I haven't seen such stupid things even in films, to say nothing about books.*

Pierre has also been forgotten. True, he is considered a genius now, but nothing has changed – his books are still not read… Yeah, it's hard to be a genius!

Paris is nice. True, I don't know anyone here yet, but it's Paris after all – the town of love; the place where people have always lost their heads – on the guillotine centuries earlier, or from love centuries later. So I will meet someone, or he will meet me… Or maybe ten years later, when Claude becomes a famous writer and makes a presentation in some bookshop, I'll go there and we will start all over again. By then he will have definitely got tired of Audrey (if they have fallen in love with each other of course) and his memories will bring him back to me. Memories are always stronger than any law of gravitation.

Bestseller

In general, everything will be exactly as it happens in films...
Oh my God, when will I finally understand that life is not a
film..."

***

"All is well that ends well," said Pierre (since if not him, then someone else would say that) and sipped the dandelion wine.

He was sitting in an armchair by the fireplace, together with Conan Doyle, and listening to the story that developed along with his own one. By then, he had already been reconciled with both his *doppelgänger* and Conan Doyle.

"Who of you is now a *doppelgänger* and who the original, that's the question."

"Now that we have finally come to an end, we shouldn't solve the riddles any more," Pierre sighed and was immediately surprised, since the situation did not require this sigh at all. "Ah, if only I could describe all this in a book, it would certainly become a bestseller."

"You can," Conan Doyle said so simply, as if it depended solely on Pierre's wish.

"?" asked Pierre's eyes.

"Very simply, life is moving forward, my friend... Do you think people are sitting idle here? We established a special staff of inspirers. We write books, then we send them with the inspirers to Earth, and they dictate them to someone there. There, on Earth, they call them muses, while here we call them just inspirers... Haven't you heard people saying about someone that he or she is influenced by Borges or Faulkner? Actually, that's not an influence but the original works by

Borges or Faulkner themselves… The main thing is to choose some kind of enthusiast for whom you would like to give your books. As for the inspirer, I promise to select the best one for you."

"Wow!" wowed Pierre for surprise or joy, "so you can observe what is happening on Earth?"

"Ha, of course! There are satellites here and we can catch any broadcaster on Earth. Did you really think that only Earth is developing in the universe?"

Pierre did, but he said nothing about it. "Hmmm, some kind of enthusiast, you say?" he repeated slowly and sipped his dandelion wine again.

***

Claude woke up at midnight. He was neither thirsty nor scared by a nightmare or some strange discomfort, so he couldn't explain what woke him up. He looked out of the window and saw no light in Audrey's apartment – she was sleeping. He felt a pleasant coolness from the fresh air and suddenly realised that a strange feeling overwhelmed him and his hands were itching. He sat down at his desk, took a sheet of paper and was about to write the same: 'Pierre Sonnage told me that when I am not able to write anything, I should write about how I can't write.'

Having written the first two words: 'Pierre Sonnage…' he paused a little, and to his amazement, continued in a different way: '…firmly decided to commit suicide on his 33rd birthday. His motivation was not banal at all…'

Bestseller

***

("It's now clear who I am," thought the Author and closed the window, since it was freezing outside and it prevented him from writing.)

***

"But if you're not a writer and you die anyway, where do you go?" asked Pierre, the second.

"Sooner or later, everyone requires an answer to this question," Poe smiled sullenly. "Do you think that there is only one Hell in the world? Everyone has their own Hell – some are grouped according to common interests; others have common characteristics or the same profession…"

"Thank god, I'm not a hard rock musician!" the second Pierre smiled too. "Why do we need such differentiation?"

"*He* thinks, there is no worse Hell in the world than sentencing like-minded people to be together forever."

"And what about paradise? Does Literary Paradise exist?"

"Paradise does, but not a Literary one, because there is no writer who hasn't tormented at least one of his readers."

The second Pierre thought about Astrid Lindgren, but he also remembered how children were forced to read books. However, he asked quite a different question:

"Are all the punishments invented by one person?"

"Yes, but it's hard to say whether he is a human or not," Poe answered and instantly realising that he had already said too much, decided to bite his tongue again.

"His salary must be very high," said Pierre like an envious earthling and sipped his calvados.

(At this point the angle of the frame changed from the shoulder level shot to the areal one, and it became obvious that Literary Hell that seemed so large was actually one of the smallest particles in the universe. Then the camera flashed across the planets, asteroids, the sun, belts, nothingness, and stopped in one small dark room.)

He was alone in the room when Big Brother appeared on the asocial network.[32]

"Have I done anything wrong?" he was worried.

"On the contrary," Big Brother was in a good mood. "I want to praise you – the punishment with the *doppelgängers* was really wonderful. You have been in this business for so long, but your devilish ingenuity has no end."

"By the way, I wanted to talk to you about that," he began meekly. "In my opinion, the time has come to free me from the centuries-long punishment of mine."

"You should not take my praise as kindness towards you," a chill crept in Big Brother's voice. "Your punishment was and will be to come up with punishments for others forever and ever!... Do you really think it's me who ought to punish everyone? Like fun! I have already developed an inferiority complex reading the Old Testament."

"But the source of my imagination is going to dry up. I no longer wish to punish anyone."

"You should have thought about it when you strove for

---

32 A special network in Literary Hell used for extremely important situations.

the highest position next to me, and forced me to punish you in this way…"

And till Lucifer managed to say another word, Big Brother disappeared from the network.

Epilogue

*"The light at the end of the tunnel might be the light of
the maternity ward where we are born."*

Pierre Sonnage, 2014, *Bestseller*

*(Then everything lit up, swirled, contracted, de-
creased to a dot and turned into a pupil of Pierre's
eye.)*

…The lift was ascending for such a long time that Pierre even
yawned three times, managed to take four selfies, hummed his
favourite tune again and again, composed the plot of a new
novel in his mind, and imagined the sentimental text (about
the ruthless world) that would occur to him during the free fall.

…And when the lift reached the place of destination,

Pierre realised that the plot of his new book was much better than that sentimental text, and that there were better ways than suicide to gain popularity. For example, he could write a book about how he writes a book about how Claude writes a book about how Pierre inspires him to write a book about Pierre. In other words, Pierre Sonnage decided to write a novel in which he himself would be a *personage*…

…And as we are all products of our childhood and head along the roads that we take or, more often, are forced to take…

…Conan Doyle was in a hurry. There was too little time and space left for writing a bestseller – about a hundred and fifty floors' distance and time respectively, that was needed for ascending from the foot of the skyscraper to its roof. The inspirer should shake his leg as well – it was not easy to inspire the plot which would make Pierre change his mind, and instead of committing suicide write a book about how Pierre wrote a book about how Claude writes a book about how Pierre inspired Claude to write a book about Pierre. But there was no other way out, since Conan Doyle's punishment was to invent extremely sophisticated plots and pass them on to hack writers who were going to commit suicide because of their lack of success. So he did his best to do it as hastily as he could…

…Lucifer was still alone in his room.

"To begin with, let him draw the Buendia family tree, and then I'll come up with something else," he told Mephistopheles. "At the moment I'm busy working on another punishment. A new one should come any minute. His name is Pierre Sonnage…"

…And Pierre, excited with the new idea, pressed the

button of the ground floor…

"…How could it be cancelled? Do they think I am sitting idle here? I'm up to my eyeballs with work!" Lucifer was indignant. He cut off communication with Mephistopheles and temporarily put the finished file of the new punishment on the shelf. "Oh my God, how many indecisive people there are in the world!"

***

"I have already started working on my fifth novel. I will complete it in about two months' time…"

Lucy was reading Pierre's interview when she received a new message in her mystical mailbox. It was from a certain Jeanne Perrisio.[33] She was very surprised, because after that stupid letter to Pierre, she no longer used that mail address…

Claude sat in his room and, as always, wrote in vain, i.e. wrote about how he could not write. He also wrote about the girl from the building opposite, who knew neither the fact that he loved her, nor anything about him. Suddenly he heard a knock on the door. Claude opened the door. There was nobody at the door, though he noticed an envelope on the floor with three words: Instructions for Claude.

…The mail had a short, simple and very banal title: 'to Lucy'. However, the addressee didn't think much about it. She opened the mail and read it:

---

33 For a logician, who from a drop of water can infer the possibility of an Atlantic or a Niagara without having seen or heard of one or the other, it will not be difficult to solve this riddle.

Bestseller

"Sundays were days off for Claude. On those days he killed no one but time and chose the next victim..."

(Curtain)

Beka Adamashvili

Recommended Reading

If you have enjoyed reading *Bestseller* you should also like the postmodernist novels of Andrew Crumey and Jean-Pierre Ohl as well as the novels of Robert Irwin:

Pfitz – Andrew Crumey
D'Alembert's Principle – Andrew Crumey
Mr Mee – Andrew Crumey
Mobius Dick – Andrew Crumey
The Secret Knowledge – Andrew Crumey
Mr Dick or The Tenth Book – Jean-Pierre Ohl
The Lairds of Cromarty – Jean-Pierre Ohl
The Arabian Nightmare – Robert Irwin
The Limits of Vision – Robert Irwin
Exquisite Corpse – Robert Irwin
Satan Wants Me – Robert Irwin

These books can be bought from your local bookshop, online from your favourite internet bookseller or direct from Dedalus. Please write to Cash Sales, Dedalus Limited, 24-26, St Judith's Lane, Sawtry, Cambs, PE28 5XE. For further details of the Dedalus list please go to our website: www.dedalusbooks.com or write to us for a catalogue or email: info@dedalusbooks.com

Pfitz – AndrewCrumey

'Rreinnstadt is a place which exists nowhere – the conception of a 18th century prince who devotes his time, and that of his subjects, to laying down on paper the architecture and street-plans of this great, yet illusory city. Its inhabitants must also be devised: artists and authors, their fictional lives and works, all concocted by different departments. When Schenck, a worker in the Cartography Office, discovers the "existence" of Pfitz, a manservant visiting Rreinnstadt, he sets about illicitly recreating Pfitz's life. Crumey is a daring writer: using the stuff of fairy tales, he ponders the difference between fact and fiction, weaving together philosophy and fantasy to create a magical, witty novel.'   *The Sunday Times*

'*Pfitz* is a surprisingly warm and likeable book, a combination of intellectual high-wire act and good traditional storytelling with a population of lovers and madmen we do care about, despite their advertised fictionality. Certainly, Crumey's narrative gymnastics have not affected his ability to create strong, fleshy characters, and none more fleshy, more fleshly, than Frau Luppen, Schenck's middle-aged landlady, a great blown rose of a woman who express her affection for her lodger by feeding him bowls of inedible stew.'

Andrew Miller in *The New York Times*

'Built out of fantasy, Andrew Crumey's novel stands, like the monumental museum at the centre of its imaginary city, as an edifice of erudition.'

Andrea Ashworth in *The Times Literary Supplement*

£8.99   ISBN   978 1 909232 80 8   146p   B. Format

Mr Dick or The Tenth Book – Jean-Pierre Ohl

'Mr Dick is a character from *David Copperfield* and Ohl's book is in many ways a homage to Dickens. It is the story of two young Frenchmen whose lives are consumed by their obsession with Dickens' life and books and in particular his final, unfinished novel, *The Mystery of Edwin Drood*. It's a playful and highly literary detective story, like a Gallic mélange of *Flaubert's Parrot* by Julian Barnes and AS Byatt's *Possession*.'   Sam Taylor in *The Observer*

'…a wonderfully inventive story of a feud between two French Drood scholars, interposed with the unreliable journal of a young Frenchman who visits Dickens just before he dies.'
                                        Andrew Taylor in *The Independent*

'The narrative Jean-Pierre Ohl's novel is flashily post-modern in technique and reminiscent of Umberto Eco's *The Name of the Rose*.'   John Sutherland in *The Financial Times*

£9.99   ISBN 978 1 903517 68 0   224p   B. Format

The Arabian Nightmare – Robert Irwin

'Robert Irwin is indeed particularly brilliant. He takes the story-within-a-story technique of the Arab storyteller a stage further, so that a tangle of dreams and imaginings becomes part of the narrative fabric. The prose is discriminating and, beauty of all beauties, the book is constantly entertaining.'

Hilary Bailey in *The Guardian*

'Robert Irwin writes beautifully and is dauntingly clever but the stunning thing about him is his originality. Robert Irwin's work, while rendered in the strictest, simplest and most elegant prose, defies definition. All that can be said is that it is a bit like a mingling of *The Thousand and One Nights* and *The Name of the Rose*. It is also magical, bizarre and frightening.'

Ruth Rendell

'At one stage in this labyrinthine narrative, a character complains "things just keep coming round in circles". The form of this clever tale owes something to *The Thousand and One Nights*. The subject matter is exotic and Eastern, the episodes linked tangentially and mingling one into another. Into the thread of the stories, Irwin injects discussions on sexuality and religion. However, since dreams, as we are shown, are themselves a deception, then the philosophical points must necessarily be falsehoods. The invention is exuberant, but the author manages to keep control to stop everything lurching into shapeless indulgence. The result is a unique and challenging fantasy.' *The Observer*

'...a classic orientalist fantasy tells the story of Balian of Norwich and his misadventures in a labyrinthine Cairo at the time of the Mamelukes. Steamy, exotic and ingenious, it is a boxes-within-boxes tale featuring such characters as Yoll, the Storyteller, Fatima the Deathly and the Father of Cats. It is a compelling meditation on reality and illusion, as well as on *Arabian Nights*-style storytelling. At its elusive centre lies the affliction of the Arabian Nightmare: a dream of infinite suffering that can never be remembered on waking, and might almost have happened to somebody else.'

Phil Baker in *The Sunday Times*

'Deft and lovely and harder to describe than to experience... the smooth steely grip of Irwin's real story-telling genius *The Arabian Nightmare* is a joy to read. If Dickens had lived to complete *The Mystery of Edwin Drood*, the full tale when told might have had something in common with the visionary urban dreamscape Robert Irwin has so joyfully unfolded in this book.'　　　　　John Clute in *The Washington Post*

£7.99　ISBN　978 1 873982 73 0　266p　B. Format

Exquisite Corpse – Robert Irwin

'*Exquisite Corpse* is among the most adventurous, ambitious and daring novels published so far this decade.'

Nicholas Royle in *Time Out*

'Robert Irwin is a master of the surreal imagination. Historical figures such as Aleister Crowley and Paul Eluard vie with fictional characters in an extended surrealist game, which, like the movement itself, is full of astonishing insights and hilarious pretensions. Superb.'

Ian Critchley in *The Sunday Times*

'*Exquisite Corpse* is one of the best novels I have read by an English person in my reading time. When I first read it I was completely bowled over.'

A.S. Byatt on Radio 4's Saturday Review

'The final chapter of the novel reads like a realistic epilogue to the book, but may instead be a hypnogogic illusion, which in turn casts doubt on many other events in the novel. Is Caroline merely a typist from Putney or the very vampire of Surrealism? It's for the reader to decide.'

Steven Moore in *The Washington Post*

£8.99   ISBN 978 1 907650 54 3   249p   B. Format